MONSTERS IN THE CLOUDS

RUSSELL JAMES

SEVERED PRESS
HOBART TASMANIA

MONSTERS IN THE CLOUDS

CHAPTER ONE

On the bright side, Grant Coleman had to acknowledge that at least today's challenges wouldn't kill him.

The line of customers snaked through the bookstore aisles and all the way to the front door. Every one held a copy of *Cavern of the Damned* and patiently awaited their turn to get the author's signature.

Grant had been at it for thirty minutes so far. A cramp plagued his hand, and his plastered-on smile threatened to crack. A book tour seemed like a soaring adventure when the publisher floated the idea. A month in, it had transformed into a grueling slog. He couldn't wait to get back to his college classroom next month.

He reminded himself it was a walk in the park compared to the real-life hell he'd endured, the events that had inspired the book. The readers loved *Cavern of the Damned*'s fantasy of giant scorpions and carnivorous bats. Grant doubted they would ever believe it had all had been reality.

A twenty-something guy in a local college T-shirt handed Grant a book from across the table. "Dr. Coleman, this is such an honor. You inspired me."

"Really?"

"Oh, yeah. The way you used real science as the basis for your novel? It really fired me up for my paleontology classes. All the creatures in the cave are completely unreal, but it's like grounded enough in fact that somehow it was like totally believable."

"Even scientists need to stretch their imaginations now and then," Grant said. "This book was just me stretching mine."

It took another hour for the line to wind down. The last customer approached as the publisher's rep and Grant's agent stepped away to talk sales numbers with the store manager. A woman Grant's age in a short red dress and black boots handed him her book. Her blonde hair was gathered in a short ponytail. The dress caught his attention, but her green eyes held it. He straightened his glasses and squared his shoulders, as if that made him seem less paunchy.

"You tell quite a story, Dr. Coleman," she said.

"It's fun to spin a little fantasy," he said. In his head it sounded flirtier than it actually did when he said it.

"But easier to just relate actualities." She opened her black leather purse and pulled out the tip of a giant cave scorpion's claw. She set it in front of him.

Grant froze. Memories of the awful days in the cave came rushing back. He'd barely escaped with his life when the cavern flooded. He didn't think any physical proof had survived. "W-where did you...?"

"We followed some rumors to a place in Montana. Found far more fact than fiction when we sifted through a creek bed there."

Grant had a bestseller under his belt. It would be a major studio blockbuster next summer. The fame had landed him a tenure-track teaching position. Any claims that he thought what he'd written had been real would brand him a crackpot, destroy all he'd built these last two years. Sweat rolled down his temple.

"Don't worry, Doctor. I'm not here to tell the world that *Cavern of the Damned* is an autobiography. I'm here to pitch your follow-up."

"What do you mean?"

She pulled a tablet from her purse and laid it on the table. With a few taps, an aerial photograph of a rainforest appeared. She pointed to a lush plateau towering over the landscape.

"My name is Thana Katsoros." She handed him a business card with the Transworld Union logo on it and a Brazilian address. "My organization just discovered this place, deep in a closed indigenous area in the Amazon rainforest. It's been isolated for who knows how long—the locals say since the world was created. Though the valley floods every year, no one climbs this plateau to escape the rising water. They say monsters rule in the clouds."

"Myths common in every culture."

She tapped the screen and magnified a specific spot on the photograph. "Tell me this is common in every culture."

Grant bent over and stared in shock.

An apatosaurus's head stuck out from the trees. Grant gasped.

"Dinosaurs, Dr. Coleman, walking the earth in a Brazilian rainforest. It takes a special kind of scientist to face down a species like that for the first time. We think your book says that scientist is you. Are we wrong?"

Grant couldn't take his eyes off the sauropod.

"No," he said. "You aren't wrong at all."

CHAPTER TWO

As he sat at his hotel room desk the next morning, Grant began his second round of second thoughts.

His initial rush of excitement had yielded to a long list of concerns. The first was the environment. He'd been a paleontologist and professor for over a decade. Field work was nothing new. But excavating dinosaurs was a very desert-oriented endeavor. Dry, quiet, and safe. Amazonian jungles were wet, loud, and dangerous. His first internet search had brought up a list of a dozen things that could kill him, from a microscopic virus to a two-hundred-pound jaguar. Katsoros and Transworld had offered him a lot of money, but he couldn't cash the check if he was dead.

Second, an apatosaurus was a little outside of his area of expertise. The average person dumped any animal that preceded *Homo sapiens* into the "prehistoric" category. That time frame was actually four billion years long and split into at least ten different periods, each with unique flora and fauna. apatosaurus's Jurassic period was about two hundred million years ahead of the Age of Mammals, his era of choice.

He'd learned one important lesson from his Montana monster hunt. Check out your supposed benefactor. The head of the expedition that ended up delivering *Cavern of the Damned* had turned out to be a con artist.

He started with an internet search for some background on Transworld Union. Pages of results popped up. This was an actual company, listed on multiple stock exchanges, the usual global conglomerate with interests in shipping, energy, pharmaceuticals, and a dozen other things that appeared unrelated. At least its check wouldn't bounce.

He searched Thana Katsoros within Transworld. An employee information page appeared. Her picture matched the person he'd met, so that was a good start. She had a business degree from a college in Greece and had been with Transworld for eleven years, currently the head of South American Exigent Product Development. The vague title did match the expedition she'd mentioned.

Her picture reminded him of the exposure Katsoros had threatened about his inspiration for *Cavern of the Damned*. He only had two semesters under his belt at the university. The dean was fine with Grant publishing fiction in his off hours, but any crazy stories about real giant scorpions would open the college up to ridicule. If Katsoros went public, he might not have a job to return to when the fall semester started next month.

Just as the decision pendulum started to swing right, to the "go for it" position, the idea of dying thrust the weight back hard to the left. Even without being stomped by a dinosaur, there were just too many ways to end up a corpse. Besides, there was no way dinosaurs had survived into the modern era.

Grant's phone rang. The caller ID read *Blood Sucking Leech*.

"Damn it." That would be Howard Berman, his ex-wife's divorce attorney. Grant could let it go to voice mail, but whenever he did, the bastard called every fifteen minutes until Grant answered. Grant pressed Accept.

"Howard, what a pleasant surprise."

"If I didn't know better," Howard said, "I'd say that was disingenuous."

"Disingenuous? Certainly not. More like a flat out lie."

"Mr. Coleman, when you choose to act as your own attorney, you get to interact with other attorneys. That's one of the perks."

Grant hadn't chosen to be his own attorney when he got divorced. Poverty had forced the decision upon him. Times like now he regretted it.

"We need to discuss the alimony," Howard said.

"I'm paid up, Howie. Since the university hired me, it's been coming straight out of my paycheck so Her Majesty can make her next yacht payment."

"Not discussing past payments. Future payments. There's a cut of author royalties she's due."

Only the expense of replacing his phone kept Grant from throwing it against the wall. "And how do you come to that conclusion?"

"The income scaling clause in the agreement, the one *you* demanded."

Grant cursed himself. His brilliant contribution to the settlement had been to have his alimony be a percent of income rather than a fixed amount. He wanted to protect himself from being thrown into debt if he ended up between teaching jobs or had to take a pay cut. He never thought he'd make any real money outside of his profession.

"I can't tell you what a pleasure it is that the two of you have been following my writing career," Grant said. "You know that book royalties don't pay much."

"No, not as much as selling those movie rights did."

"Son of a bitch," Grant whispered to himself. Grant had only found out about the rights sale last week. "No way she deserves a cut of this, Howzer. I did all this work after we were divorced."

"Feel free to fight the modification," Howard said. "You'll lose and I'll tack my legal billing to the alimony, as well as the accrued interest from the delay. Think on that and we'll get together when you get back from this little tour."

"Don't you think sleeping with my ex-wife creates a conflict of interest in handling her divorce?"

"If that slanderous accusation was true, which it isn't, I'd think it would just make for a more zealous advocate. Talk to you soon."

Howard hung up. Grant again beat back the impulse to destroy his phone.

This little bit of extortion would be expensive to fight. But he was going to fight it, and with an actual lawyer on his side this time. He might lose, but he'd take a pound of flesh from Howard and the ex-wife doing it. Pyrrhic victories didn't come cheap though.

Lucky for him, he had a chance to make a little money in the Amazon.

The dino-decision pendulum swung back full right, and he searched his papers for Katsoros's business card.

CHAPTER THREE

Transworld Union's Brazilian headquarters rose from São Paulo's streets and towered over Janaina Silva. Gleaming steel and mirrored glass stretched up so high she had to crane her neck to see the top. Glass elevators surged up and down the outside of the building.

The dark blue business suit she'd borrowed from her roommate complemented her olive skin, but it wasn't providing the hoped for comfort in this corporate environment. The unfamiliar clothing just made her seem even more out of place, inside strange clothes outside a strange building. If Transworld's goal was to make her feel intimidated by meeting here, they had scored.

Transworld's business with her was a mystery. Her supervisor at the Native People's Foundation said that Transworld had requested a representative to advise them on potential contact with indigenous people in a remote section of the Amazon. They'd specifically asked for Mariel Castro, but the woman had a last-minute emergency with her granddaughter. Since Mariel had turned sixty, she'd become more family-than-work focused. Janaina had been called an hour ago to fill in, and she wasn't even certain what she'd be filling in for.

She took a deep breath. Whatever Transworld wanted, she was up for it. She'd been defending the rights of the aboriginal people of the jungle for years. Not against a company as formidable as Transworld Union, but experience showed that with right on her side, might had always seemed to follow. She had to have faith it would again. She swept her black hair behind her shoulders and then straightened her jacket. With a swirl of the revolving doors, she entered the air conditioning.

Five minutes and a dizzying elevator ride later, Janaina stood alone in the office of Thana Katsoros. The title on the door read Director of Exigent Product Development, whatever that meant.

Katsoros entered. Janaina was several centimeters taller than Katsoros, but the woman with the short blonde hair and the piercing green eyes didn't seem like the type who let height intimidate her. She wore dark pants, heels, a white open blouse, and a look of surprise.

"Who are you?" she asked.

Katsoros's default to English irritated Janaina. If the woman was going to work in Brazil with Brazilians, she should speak Portuguese, no matter what language was standard in her more international office. She set the slight aside and extended a hand.

"I am Janaina Silva from the Fundação dos Povos Nativos." She hoped using her organization's Portuguese title would remind Katsoros that she was in Brazil. "We have a meeting at one o'clock."

Katsoros left Janaina's hand hanging in space and walked around her to the desk. She shuffled through some papers until she found a resume from Mariel. "What happened to Ms. Castro?"

"Family emergency. I am here in her place."

Katsoros gave her a dismissive look. "I'd asked for someone with more experience."

Janaina bristled. "I have been with the Foundation for almost ten years. I *am* experienced."

Katsoros waved for Janaina to take the seat in front of her desk. Janaina sat down.

"Transworld Union has purchased the rights to several hundred acres in Amazonia," Katsoros said. "We'll be scouting the area for two weeks."

"Scouting for what?"

"Natural resources, undiscovered plants for pharmaceuticals, solar or hydropower locations. We are a diverse company."

That sounded like a load of crap to Janaina. Multinationals didn't invest big bucks unless they had a specific, profitable, agenda.

"The government would prefer we had an expert on the indigenous peoples on staff," Katsoros continued, "in the event we come across any isolated tribes. We will set you up with an office here so you can advise us if needed."

"I am not understanding this."

"We have complete satellite phone capability. If we come across any locals, we'll contact you. There's no point in you having to endure all the hardships of the jungle when it's so unlikely we'll encounter anyone."

"That is not the right procedure."

"The arrangement has been cleared by the Interior Ministry."

Janaina's confusion boiled into fury as she put the pieces together. Transworld had bribed someone to okay this ridiculous setup. Katsoros had asked for Maria because Katsoros knew the older woman would welcome such a cushy gig. No company would go to all that effort unless it wanted to keep something secret. Janaina stood up.

"I don't know who would be saying that arrangement would be acceptable, but it is not. I will accompany your team into the Amazon."

Katsoros opened a folder on her desk and looked at the first page. "No you won't. I can hire someone else who will find the arrangement not only acceptable, but preferable."

Janaina whipped out her phone and called up a recent news article. She put her phone down over the paper Katsoros was reading. "Do you remember this?"

Katsoros slid the phone closer. The article was about how timber company Empresa de Madeiras Cruz do Sul had carved a logging road into some protected land. Protesters had ringed the headquarters. Builders promised to boycott the company's timber. The stock price dropped. The company backed down.

"Yes, I saw that last year."

Janaina yanked back her phone. "How would you like for Transworld Union to get that treatment this year? Except that was a local company. Your bad press would be international. I will not let you be compromising native peoples, and then cover it up."

Katsoros's eyes narrowed in anger. Then her face relaxed into an artificial smile. "There's no need for all this hostility. We just thought it would be easier on you to remain back as a consultant. There's plenty of room on the transport if you would rather go into the field."

"I most certainly will."

"We leave at dawn from Virocopos Airport."

"Tomorrow?"

Virocopos was outside Campinas, a hundred kilometers of gridlocked São Paulo traffic away. Janaina didn't have a car. She hadn't packed, wasn't even certain she had what she needed to pack for such a trip.

"If that's not enough notice, I completely understand." Katsoros turned back to the folder on the desk.

"Oh, no. It is no problem. I'll be there."

"Then I guess I'll see you in the morning. Hangar Three."

Janaina was so furious she stomped out of Katsoros' office. All the way down in the elevator she fumed about Katsoros's arrogance and Transworld's obvious deceit. Only when the elevator approached the ground floor did she comprehend the scared looks on the faces of everyone else in the car. She realized she must look the way she felt—ready for a fight.

And Katsoros was going to get one. No native people were going to be sacrificed for Transworld Union.

***

Katsoros watched the security feed and saw Janaina leave the building. She picked up the phone and dialed three numbers.

"We have a complication. A replacement for Mariel Castro demands to go into the field."

"That increases the risk of our secrets going public," a deep voice responded.

"I'll make certain that it doesn't. Amazonia can be dangerous. People die out there all the time."

CHAPTER FOUR

Grant Coleman staggered off his flight and into the São Paulo airport. A variety of minor problems had added up to a major delay in his arrival. His brain was too fuzzy to do the math, but he thought he'd been awake for twenty hours.

After gathering his bags at baggage claim, he turned to see a stout man in a black suit carrying a tablet with "Dr. Grant Coleman" and a Transworld Union logo glowing on its screen. Grant sighed with relief because upon landing he'd realized that he spoke no Portuguese and his only contact for Transworld Union was through a United States phone number.

"I'm Dr. Coleman," Grant told the man.

The man smiled with the same level relief Grant felt. "Good." He patted his chest. "Hervé."

"Hey, Hervé."

"We go airport now."

Grant was going to correct him that we were going from the airport now, but he was too tired and too happy that Hervé's minimal English made up for Grant's complete lack of Portuguese. Hervé grabbed Grant's roller bag, and Grant followed him through the terminal.

They passed outside to a parking garage and the humid night air hit him like a boxer's jab. He cringed thinking that he wasn't even in the jungle yet, and São Paulo was comparatively temperate. Hervé loaded his bag into the trunk of a black four-door Mercedes. Grant plopped into the rich, leather back seat. He was asleep before Hervé got out of the garage.

***

"Doctor!"

Grant came to with Hervé nudging him from the open door of the car. It was still night time. Grant checked his watch and saw two hours had passed. "Yes. Okay. Thank you."

He slid out of the car with his backpack and stood up. An older-style aircraft hangar stared him in the face.

"Hervé, where are we?"

"We go airport."

"No, we go hotel. Sleep, Shower. Food."

"You late. No hotel. Aeroporto Virocopos." Hervé dropped Grant's bag beside him, got back into the Mercedes, and drove away.

A beefy security guard approached from under the hangar lights. He wasn't a mall cop. A stubby sub-machine gun hung from his shoulder across his Kevlar vest.

A heavily-armed man on a dark taxiway at an unknown airport, Grant thought. *Great.*

His anxiety dialed up again about his lack of Portuguese language skills. He stood stock still and hoped against reason that might make him invisible.

"Dr. Coleman?" the guard said in American English.

Grant managed a relieved "Yes."

"You're late."

"I've heard that."

"This way."

Grant followed him to a door beside the main hangar door. The guard typed in a code on a keypad and the door unlocked. He opened it.

The inside of the hangar was almost as dark as it was outside. A few emergency exit signs at the far end provided some scant illumination. The dark mass of a large aircraft filled most of the space. Shadowy lumps of people slept in neat rows on foldable, canvas cots. Stacks of equipment sat by the rear of the plane.

"Get some sleep," the guard said. He pointed Grant to an empty cot. "The plane leaves at dawn."

"How many hours from now is that?"

"Do you really want to know?"

Grant decided that he didn't. He stepped inside and the guard closed the door behind him. The snap of the lock echoed in the cavernous space. A light drone of snoring rose from the group. Grant shuffled to the open cot and set down his bags. He lay on the cot and before he could take off his shoes, he fell sound asleep.

CHAPTER FIVE

Dawn ended up being four hours away. But the hangar lights flared on an hour earlier. It felt like they set Grant's retinas on fire. He forced himself out of the cot.

The rest of the hangar looked like someone had kicked over an anthill. People scurried back and forth, closing containers, trussing up bags, and checking the enormous aircraft in the hangar's center.

A squat C-130 transport plane in faded green camouflage pointed toward the closed hangar door. Markings from its former military career were spray painted over in flat black. Two giant prop engines hung from each side of the overhead wing. An open ramp at the rear exposed an interior already packed with pallets. He could see the one closest to the door, but the nature of the packed items was obscured by layers of opaque stretch wrapping.

An announcement spat from an overhead speaker. "Briefing in five."

Grant had the sudden realization that this might be his last access to running water for a while. He spent the next four minutes in the bathroom with a toothbrush and soap. Then he followed the traffic that headed into a room off the main hangar.

A lanky man in faded Vietnam-era jungle fatigues stood at the front of the room. His shaved head had the shape of a bullet, and from the semi-permanent scowl on his face, Grant thought that might be why he'd shaved it. A dozen people filled the irregular rows of folding chairs that faced him.

"Listen up!" the man bellowed.

The room went silent.

"I'm Jason McCabe," he said. "I'm running insertion, extraction, and on-the-ground security for this op. We're going someplace dangerous and we are not taking some pansy-ass cruise to get there."

All of Grant's misgivings about this trip knocked on the inside of his head and said "I told you so."

"If at any moment during this op," McCabe continued, "I take time out of my busy day to talk to you, it's because what I'm telling you to do will save your life. So don't ask questions, just do it."

McCabe looked around the room as if daring someone to object. None did.

"We are wheels up in forty-five," he said. "So if your gear isn't packed and stowed you are way behind the power curve. Ms. Katsoros will give the overview, then I'll talk details."

He stepped aside and Thana Katsoros stood up and took his place. She wore khaki cargo pants, combat boots, and a baggy blue T-shirt. This was certainly the woman who recruited him at the book signing, but she sure didn't look the same. Even the scarf tied around her neck had a patina that said it had been put to productive, rather than decorative, use during its lifetime. She'd cut off the blonde ponytail since they'd last met, no doubt a concession to the jungle. She tapped a laptop keyboard and a projector lit up the wall behind her.

"This is the first time all parts of the team are together, so I'm taking the opportunity to make certain you all know the roles you will be playing over the next two weeks."

She tapped up an aerial picture of a forested plateau rising from a misty jungle. Another layer of clouds capped it from the sky above.

"This is our destination, deep in the protected lands in Amazonia state. This three-hundred-square-kilometer plateau rises about a hundred meters above the jungle floor, with the headwaters of the Amazon flowing around it. The combination of mist below, clouds above, and general middle-of-nowhere isolation have kept the place unknown and unexplored."

"By Europeans," said a woman from the front row. She was tall, with angular features and dark hair that just passed her shoulders. She wore a black military style shirt that looked at least a size too large.

"Explored by anyone," Katsoros said with irritation. "There is the slim possibility of indigenous tribes in the area, completely isolated from outside contact. But the plateau's sheer cliffs guarantee that no locals have climbed up there. It would be technologically impossible. However, to placate the government and to prove our point, we've enlisted, at our expense, Ms. Janaina Silva," Katsoros made a dismissive hand gesture to the woman in the black shirt, "of the Native People's Foundation to certify the obvious."

Janaina turned and gave the group a smile that was not returned. Hers wilted and she turned back around. Grant's heart went out to her.

"Now what sparked the attention of Transworld Union was this picture." Katsoros switched photos to the one she had shown Grant when they met. An apatosaurus head stuck out from a tree line at the edge of a cliff.

"We believe that this picture shows that animals from the age of the dinosaurs have survived in this isolated microclimate. This expedition will prove it. But we have no plan to turn it into some version of Jurassic Park. We all know how that ends."

The room filled with nervous laughter.

"Transworld Union just wants the genetic makeup. These could be the keys that unlock the world of millions of years ago, codes that can help cure disease, extend life, answer questions about how these animals lived, and maybe why they died. To help on that end we've brought renowned expert on extinct animals, Dr. Grant Coleman."

She pointed to Grant at the rear of the room. He straightened his glasses and gave them a sheepish wave. A look of recognition crossed the face of a swarthy bearded man in a Korn T-shirt and baggy jeans.

"Wait a minute," he said. "Didn't you write that book about the giant scorpions in a cave?"

Crap, Grant thought. *Of all the times to meet a fan.* "Well, yes."

"Ain't that kind of like making Tom Hanks an astronaut because he played one in a movie?"

Grant bristled. "I have three degrees, including a doctorate in paleontology. I've spent a decade of summers in field excavations. I've taught at several colleges. I know what I'm talking about when it comes to extinct species."

Okay, he'd puffed that resume up about ten percent. But the guy pissed him off, and no one would be doing any background checks at this point.

"Dr. Coleman has more than proven himself in expeditions such as this," Katsoros said. "Transworld has complete faith in him."

She pointed to a man one seat behind Janaina. "Our other scientist is Dr. Kabir Dixit. He's our biologist who will be extracting that DNA."

Dr. Dixit was practically round, with a thick mop of black hair and skin the color of light chocolate. Grant didn't think that he looked old enough to have earned a doctorate, but fifteen-year-olds were taking college classes online now, so what did he know.

"He's going to swab the mouth of the dinosaur for DNA?" Grant said. The smart-ass quip slipped out before he could stop it. The room laughed again.

"No, no," Dixit said. His Indian accent was thick. "My technician Mr. Hobart and I can sample quite passively in a multitude of ways, such as from eggshells, shed skin, or urine deposits and fecal matter."

Grant made a mental note to skip the fecal matter sampling.

A geeky-looking kid in bifocal glasses and an eruption of acne sat behind Dixit. He listened to Dixit with the intensity only a lackey could muster, so he had to be Dixit's tech. Hobart had "fecal matter sampler" stamped all over him.

"And to make certain everyone gets home safe," Katsoros said, "Mr. McCabe and his men will be, as he said, providing security for us. Mr. Griggs and Mr. Riffaud are his team. All ex-military and expert marksmen, they will be there to defend us from any attack."

Two other men in jungle fatigues leaned against the body of the plane. Both had automatic rifles slung over their shoulder. Riffaud was the taller of the two, with sallow cheeks, high cheekbones and black hair shorn down to stubble. Griggs had longer dark hair and a reddish moustache that melted down both sides of his mouth past his chin. Griggs gave a two-finger salute.

An apatosaurus was herbivorous, but after fighting giant bats and scorpions in the Montana cavern, Grant wasn't going to complain about having some defensive firepower on his side.

"Mr. McCabe?" Katsoros moved aside and McCabe stepped up.

"My mission is to get you in and out in one piece," McCabe said. "To get in, I'd use a helicopter. But the distance is too great, the cargo too heavy. So we are going to fly in using that C-130."

Grant raised an eyebrow. He didn't see a runway in the pictures Katsoros showed them.

"We'll be airdropping the expedition from a thousand feet up into a meadow to the northeast."

Grant's eyes went wide.

"The supply pallet will drop first, the equipment pallet will drop last. All non-jump qualified personnel will drop in the cargo container on the middle pallet."

Oh, hell no, Grant thought.

A picture of the inside of a container about the size of a one-car garage popped up. It had no windows though it looked like mesh-covered vents made up the top quarter of the walls. Uncomfortable, upright plastic seats on springs lined each side, facing in. Each seat had what looked like a race car's four-point safety harness.

"We'll make one pass over the DZ, then on the second, everyone will take their seat. The door locks automatically when it closes. Buckle in and stay seated. If you get up and run around like a damn fool during the drop, you'll screw up the CG and the box will land ass over elbows. We've done this dozens of times. It works perfectly when you follow instructions."

"No one mentioned parachuting," Janaina said, almost to herself.

From the looks on the faces of the non-military team members, McCabe's explanation wasn't reassuring anyone else either. The pilot and co-pilot looked at each other and laughed at the big joke on the passengers.

Of course they'd think it's funny, Grant thought. *They're going to fly back here and drive home.*

"My men and I will jump in solo. We'll get you out when you land and make certain the area is secure. Stay in the container until we give the all clear. There is a small electric Bobcat front loader on the third pallet. Mr. Griggs will use it to clear a landing strip for our extraction at mission's end."

"Transworld wouldn't have okayed this if they didn't think it was safe," Katsoros said. "I mean, I'm in the box with you, right?"

"That's it," McCabe said. "Gather your gear, meet on the ramp when the aircraft is out of the hangar."

The pilots and the military escort headed out the door. Grant approached Dixit, figuring the most likely to bond with on this excursion would be the fellow scientist.

"Well, parachuting wasn't in the cruise brochure," Grant said to him. "Do you think they'll charge us extra for it later?"

"Come again?" Dixit said.

Grant feared a translation issue. "Don't worry about it. Just wanted to say I'm glad there'll be another man of science on the ground."

Dixit gave him a sideways look. "One man of science. One storyteller."

So that's how this is going down, Grant thought. "Well, great talking to you. Have fun collecting the feces. I prefer mine fossilized. If you come across some of those, let me know."

Grant grabbed his bag and headed out through the open hangar door. The ground crew was hooking a tug to a tow pole secured to the nose of the C-130. False dawn lit the edge of the eastern sky.

He realized by the time the sun was straight overhead, he could be face to face with a living dinosaur.

CHAPTER SIX

Once the whining hydraulics closed the rear ramp, Grant realized that the C-130 had no windows in the cargo area. Not that the palletized cargo needed them, but the human cargo might want a reminder that there was daylight out there.

Dim electric lights lit the cargo bay. Gray pads of insulation covered the interior of the fuselage. A row of inward-facing canvas-mesh seats ran along each side of the aircraft. Grant had to suck in his belly to pass the pallets and sit down. He was pleased to see the rotund Dixit go through much more of a struggle. An orange and white Bobcat front loader sat strapped to the third pallet. Dried mud still clung to its twin tank treads. Right next to it, a seat beside Janaina was open. Dixit wasn't going to be a good field trip buddy. Chatting up one of the mercenaries was off the table. He hoped Janaina might be a better fit.

He plopped down in the seat. His butt felt like a waffle as the latticework of canvas straps compressed strips of his cheeks.

"That's comfortable," he said to no one in particular but he hoped to Janaina in specific.

"Three hours from now," she said, "I may be permanently numb from nerve damage."

"That will work to our advantage if a dinosaur bites us in the butt."

"Dinosaurs. You are not thinking we'll really see any, are you?"

"The pictures seem legit." He thought about the cave from Hell in Montana. "And stranger things have happened. Trust me. Don't you think there might be dinosaurs?"

"Hardly. What I do think is that there will be indigenous tribes, possibly with no previous contact with the outside world. My job is to keep them protected."

"I hadn't considered there might be human beings there, and from the start I assumed there were dinosaurs. You believe the opposite. Odds are only one of us can be right."

"Soon enough," she said, "we will know for sure."

"Given the quality of our seating, it can't possibly be soon enough."

"The time will pass fast as thunder."

"Lightning."

"Lightning?"

"The phrase is 'fast as lightning'."

"Ah, some of your phrases, they don't translate easily. I'm still trying them out."

Outside, engines sputtered to life. By the time the fourth one spun up to speed, conversation was impossible. Between the echoing roar and the vibrations through the hull, Grant felt like he was in a rock tumbler. Exhaust fumes seeped into the aircraft.

McCabe banged on one of the steel ribs of the plane with a crowbar and the clang managed to rise above the din. He wore a bulky headset. He tapped it and pointed to the area above everyone's head. Headsets hung over each of them, though only McCabe's had a mic. Grant snapped his on. Blessedly, it cut the roar of the engines down to a rumble.

"Okay, everyone can hear me now," McCabe said. "Stay seated and strapped in. It's going to be loud, it's going to be warm, it's going to be uncomfortable. Boo hoo. Above all, keep these on. When we get to the DZ I'll give you instructions to load up for the drop. Miss that announcement and you may still be on board when everyone else exits."

Compared to being strapped in a box and thrown out the back of a perfectly good airplane, Grant didn't consider that to be such a bad alternative.

***

The next three hours passed as McCabe had promised—loud, warm, and uncomfortable. The good news was that Grant managed to nod off for most of it. The bad news was that he woke up needing to pee.

McCabe's voice came over the headset. "We're arriving at the plateau. Listen for my order to prepare for insertion."

Down at the loading ramp, Griggs stood and strapped on a parachute.

Grant's bladder made another, stronger cry for relief. McCabe's earlier welcome message hadn't included any mention of an inflight bathroom, but Grant reasoned that there had to be one. Even without passengers, the crew would be flying for six hours. Surely they didn't resort to empty soda bottles?

He hung his headset back on the wall, unbuckled his seat belt and tottered to the front of the aircraft. The door to the cockpit stood open, with the flight deck a few steps higher than the cargo area. Curiosity took hold, and Grant stepped up into the doorway.

The two pilots sat at the controls. Through the windshields Grant saw plateau like in the pictures. It rose like an island from a sea of white fog. Trepidation and exhilaration sparred as he worried about parachuting in and anticipated what waited below in that unexplored land. The plane flew over the plateau.

Suddenly, something big and brown slammed through the co-pilot's windshield. The cockpit exploded into a maelstrom of blasting, roaring wind. The mass of whatever it was sliced into the co-pilot's neck and decapitated him. His severed head smashed into the bulkhead next to Grant.

Alarms blared. Warning lights bathed the cockpit in red. Something exploded outside along the starboard wing and the plane lurched right.

Grant lost his grip and sailed into the starboard bulkhead. His head hit metal and he saw stars. The plane snapped back level and he slid to the cargo bay floor. His head swam as he sat up.

The roar of the air through the smashed windshield obliterated any other noise, so the cargo area looked like a high-speed silent movie. Griggs dropped the cargo ramp and the airflow now rushed straight through the aircraft like a wind tunnel. Riffaud snapped some of the cargo straps free on the first pallet. McCabe rushed all the non-military personnel from the uncomfortable mesh seats into the drop container. He'd donned his parachute as well.

Grant realized he was about to be left behind.

He pulled himself to his feet. At the door of the personnel carrier, Janaina pointed over McCabe's shoulder at Grant. McCabe ignored her and shoved her into the box.

Griggs released the last cargo strap on the first pallet. It slid down the ramp and out of the aircraft. A static line pulled the parachute open and the load disappeared from view. Griggs tightened his rifle to his chest and leapt out the open door.

The plane lurched left. The door to the personnel container slammed shut. Grant careened across the cargo floor and slammed into the port side exit door. The handle poked him hard in the side and added another bruise to his growing collection.

The plane leveled, but the sinking feeling in Grant's middle ear said it was still falling. McCabe pulled a knife from his belt and slashed the cargo straps on the personnel pallet. He shoved it forward and it rolled toward the gaping opening in the aircraft's rear. McCabe spun and cut the straps on the Bobcat's pallet. The personnel carrier dropped out of the ramp and the parachute deployed. The Bobcat pallet started to roll toward McCabe. He sprinted for the door and dove through head first.

The plane rocked again. The nose rose and fell as the pilot struggled for altitude. The last pallet stopped rolling. Grant was no expert, but this had all the earmarks of an impending crash.

Riding it out would be suicide. There weren't any spare parachutes hanging on the bulkhead. There was only one potentially safe way to the ground, and it was about to roll out the door.

Grant ran for the Bobcat.

He caught up with it as it resumed rolling toward the ramp. Fueled by adrenaline, he bounded onto the front bucket and dropped through the cage into the seat. The pallet accelerated toward the open ramp. Grant snapped the seatbelt around his waist, and immediately wondered what good that would possibly do. He clamped his hands to the sides of the cage and held his breath.

The pallet rolled out the ramp and all Grant saw was blue sky.

Then the pallet rotated forward, and all he saw was jungle. And it was coming up fast.

CHAPTER SEVEN

The parachute's static line uncoiled like a snake from the top of the Bobcat as it plummeted down. With a *thunk* it snapped tight and released the chute. Nylon whipped against nylon as the canopy deployed. Grant's terrified focus stayed glued on the approaching ground.

Wind caught the chute and it popped wide open. The pallet leveled and Grant compressed into the seat as the descent jerked to a slower speed.

Slower, but nowhere near slow. The closer he came to the ground, the faster it seemed to approach. A rolling meadow, no doubt the original intended landing strip, lay kilometers away. A kilometer or more in front of him floated the other pallet and the personnel carrier. It looked like they had a fighting chance of making a small burned-over clearing at the jungle's edge. The three individual parachutes of the military team followed them down from above.

Below him stretched nothing but trees. Even if he could steer this sinking ship, he could never get to the clearing before impact.

From somewhere behind him came the scream of engines and then a crash and a boom. The C-130 had probably spiraled in. But Grant didn't have time to look. Treetops were coming up fast. A quick death aboard the C-130 might have been a better option.

The last thirty meters of the drop came at high speed. Suddenly it seemed like he could count the leaves on the trees. Then he was in them.

The pallet burst through the jungle like a plow through snow. Animals screamed warnings from the jungle around him as the pallet sent leaves and branches flying like a noisy, earth-colored blizzard. Tree limbs snapped like toothpicks.

The parachute caught on the treetops and shredded into streamers. The pallet dropped like a stone. Grant closed his eyes and prayed.

The pallet slammed into the earth. The Bobcat compressed its springs and bottomed out against the steel. Grant's body yanked forward into an L around his seatbelt. His jaw slammed his knee in a feat of flexibility he didn't know he'd possessed. Teeth sliced lip and blood flowed.

Then all went silent. He tasted warm copper. Grant opened one eye, then the other. His spine made a creaking noise as he sat up. He exhaled.

"Still not dead," he muttered in amazement.

He unclicked the seatbelt and gave the buckle a caress. "Seat belts save lives."

The pallet sat in a clearing. Seconds before it hadn't been so, but the plummeting pallet had made short work of the rain forest. Hazy sunlight through the cloud cover illuminated the ground around him.

A quick self-diagnostic told him he hadn't broken anything save the skin where he'd tried to bite through his lip on impact. He'd been lucky.

Now if this were a movie, he'd fire up the Bobcat, and then clear himself a way through the jungle to the others. This not being a movie, he had no key for the Bobcat and didn't know how to drive it if he had one. He gave brief consideration to the idea of sitting here until someone came to the rescue. They would likely be in search of the Bobcat instead of him, but it would all be the same in the end.

But what if Janaina or Katsoros were in that rescue party, hacking through the jungle while he sat here in a cushioned vinyl seat? That was a big bite of manhood surrender that he wasn't about to swallow.

He climbed down and stepped on the spongy earth. It crossed his mind that he was the first human being to set foot on this particular spot. It was like the feeling he had when he unearthed a fossil after it had been buried a few million years. Except that this sensation was more visceral, more alive.

Then he remembered the last time he'd felt this way, in the Montana cavern, where every creature he encountered wanted to kill him.

He set out in the direction of the burned over clearing, and the safety of numbers.

***

Two hours and multiple scratches and bumps later, he stepped out into the clearing. The scent of char tinged the air. Though the clearing looked wide open from the air, at ground level it was obvious that the lightning had only caused a flash fire. While the canopy and the underbrush had turned to cinders, the larger trees still stood like stripped, blackened sentinels. In no time, the regenerative power of the forest would no doubt heal this wound. Out west he could see the high ground further out on the plateau.

Off to the left, the personnel carrier lay on its side, one of the twin doors wide open. Its parachute draped across the ground like a deflated balloon. He had a bad feeling the box was full of corpses. He shifted to a less morbid train of thought, that maybe someone inside might need help. He ran to the open door.

He stuck his head inside. It was dark, but he could make out the seats on both sides. All empty. No corpses. He sighed.

He stepped away from the container and practically ran into Griggs. Startled, he let out a little yelp.

"Where'd you come from?" Griggs said.

"Originally, Salt Lake City."

Griggs didn't look amused.

"I hitched a ride on the pallet with the Bobcat," Grant said

"The Bobcat made it? Where?"

"Why yes, I'm fine. Thanks for asking. And the Bobcat is about a mile north of this clearing. Where are the others?"

"This way."

Griggs led him out of the clearing and into the jungle. A hundred yards in, the survivors from the plane were unloading the other pallet.

From the looks of the gap in the canopy, it had crash landed about as well as the Bobcat. Maybe worse. Several cracked containers had spewed their contents all over the jungle. He searched faces until he found Janaina. She looked uninjured. That made him smile. Getting hurt on a trip where no one wanted her in the first place would just make her even more miserable. Grant did a head count and came up one short.

Then he noticed the missing person. Riffaud sat up about fifteen feet in the crook of a tree, scanning the area with binoculars, automatic rifle lying across two branches beside him.

Griggs walked Grant over to McCabe, who was studying a map.

"Located the Bobcat," Griggs said.

McCabe looked up, right past Grant without pause, and locked eyes on Griggs. "You're kidding? Damage report?"

Grant wedged his face in front of McCabe. "Still in one piece. As am I. Seriously, you two need to stop gushing over my survival."

McCabe pushed Grant back with one finger. "And where the hell were you when everything went sideways?"

"Standing by the cockpit, looking for a restroom." He realized he no longer needed to go. He didn't want to know why. "Something crashed into the windshield and killed one of the pilots."

"And then from the sound of it, we lost at least one engine," McCabe said. "Probably a bird strike at the low level we were flying."

"Since no planes have ever been here," Grant said, "birds would have no clue about aircraft. They couldn't judge the speed and avoid one."

Grant was pretty proud of his insightful addition to the conversation. McCabe looked not only unimpressed, but possibly irritated. He turned back to Griggs. "Take one of the science geeks and go find the Bobcat. It should have enough juice to get back here. By then we'll have the solar panels up for recharging."

McCabe headed over to Riffaud's tree and began to brief him on what Griggs was doing. Janaina saw Grant and rushed over.

"*Ai, meu Deus!* We were all thinking you were dead. How did you get here?"

"I drove the Bobcat."

She looked at him in confusion.

"I mean, not the whole way, obviously. I got it from the plane to the ground. That's the hard part, right? Griggs is leaving to bring it the rest of the way here. I'll let him have his moment."

"I... I don't know how much of what you are saying is a joke."

"Then we'll get along splendidly."

Katsoros approached the group with a satellite phone in her hand. "This thing didn't survive the drop. We have no communication back to Transworld." She gave Grant a double-take. "Dr. Coleman! We were afraid that you went down with the plane."

"Only half of the way," Grant said.

McCabe returned. "Did you see where it crashed?"

"Northeast of here somewhere."

"That matches the location of a smoke plume earlier. Wasn't sure if that was the plane or a fire like the one that burned this place over."

"Hate to be a downer after surviving the crash," Grant said. "But with no way to call home, how do we get out of here?"

"Plan B," Katsoros said. "Any loss in communications and a rescue team launches in seventy-two hours."

"Maybe earlier when the C-130 doesn't return," McCabe said.

"Then we do what we came to do until then," Katsoros said. "It looks like we have the basics we need to do it."

Griggs corralled Dixit and Hobart, and told Dixit he was taking Hobart to get the Bobcat. Dixit nodded and began searching an open equipment container. Griggs frog-marched Hobart westward.

"Dixit seems more worried about his equipment than that his assistant just got sent into an uncharted jungle, maybe filled with dinosaurs," Janaina said.

"Maybe Hobart's gift is the dino poo collecting," Grant said. "As long as he's back in time for that..."

Janaina knit her brow. "What is, how you say, 'poo'?"

"Pretty much most of my conversation. Just let it slide."

***

30

Two hours later, the setting sun backlit the Bobcat as it rolled out of the jungle. It appeared that it also brought a good deal of the jungle wrapped around it. A silent electric motor instead of a growling diesel engine made the arrival even more surreal. Hobart hung from the back, looking over the cage with a big goofy grin. Grant thought that Hobart likely didn't get out of the lab much.

By now everyone had sorted their items and inventoried their losses. Grant had brought the least, just some basics in a backpack, but had lost the most of anyone: all of it. In the humidity he already smelled more gamey than he preferred. This was going to be a long trip. With few friends.

He did find the fossil-hunting kit he'd shipped ahead to Transworld. He wasn't sure what they'd find while they were here, but while others searched for living fossils, he didn't want to be caught flat-footed if they happened across any Triassic-era versions.

Griggs pulled the Bobcat up to the toppled personnel carrier. He used the bucket loader to lift one edge and set the box upright with a crash.

They spent the time until dusk ferrying everything from the crashed pallet to the container in the bucket loader. There they set up one area for supplies and another by the rear of the container as a work area for Dixit and Hobart. Riffaud even fashioned a sunshade out of some tree limbs and one of the parachutes. After the early start, the adrenaline rush of the crash, and the exercise setting up the base camp, everyone was exhausted.

"Listen up!" McCabe called out. "It's almost dark. We don't know what's out here, but whatever's here will be curious about the creatures that crashed down from the sky. I want any meetings we have with the local wildlife to be on my terms, not theirs. The most secure place is the big box, so you are all going in. My men and I will stand guard in rotation so you can all sleep without worry."

"And how are we to all sleep in such a place?" Dixit said. His clipped, accented delivery was exceptionally shrill. "There is no room to lie down."

"Sitting up and strapped in," McCabe said. "Or you can sleep out here with the unknown. See if it has a taste for human flesh. I'll try to kill it before it eats you, but it'll be dark and I make no guarantees."

Dixit's lips quivered. "Sitting up it is, then."

The group trudged to the box, Hobart on Dixit's heels, Katsoros right behind them. Janaina followed her. Grant was torn between wanting to sit next to her and fearing having his scent repel her if he did. He decided to chance it and followed her in.

The mesh along the sides let some more-than-welcome air pass through. Everyone took a seat and strapped in. Riffaud and Griggs took the seats on either side of the door. McCabe swung it shut. The waning sunlight barely lit the interior through the screens. The men propped their rifles against the side of the container, leaned back in the seats, and were almost instantly asleep. The rest of the team quickly followed suit.

He tucked his glasses into his pocket for safe-keeping. Tired as he was, the anticipation of what lay ahead tomorrow gave Grant a mental rush that made sleep elusive. He might be face-to-face with a dinosaur in hours.

CHAPTER EIGHT

Grant's morning revelation was that if he was tired enough, he could sleep sitting upright strapped into a rock-hard seat. He sighed with relief, because he had at least two more nights of it ahead of him. He put his glasses on and brought the world back into focus.

As he got up, he felt the impact. He was stiff as hell. Between sticking the landing in the Bobcat yesterday and a full night of pressure on his spine, his back felt like he'd borrowed every vertebra from an octogenarian.

Rosy sunlight shined through the half-open container door. Dixit and Hobart hung forward against their straps, with Dixit emitting a stuttering snore. Griggs also still slept in a seat by the door, but everyone else had already escaped the box.

Grant stretched and stepped outside. The air still held the cool of the night and a slight breeze made it a bit chilly. McCabe and the others were gathered around the containers from the first pallet, eating breakfast out of brown pouches. Janaina smiled and approached him carrying two of the little sacks.

"Coffee and croissant?" Janaina asked.

"I was more in the mood for the brown pouch special," Grant said.

Janaina handed him one. "Then it is your lucky day."

"That was my first thought as I awakened in my torture chair."

"Wasn't it awful? I woke myself up from my snoring. I am so embarrassed."

"I didn't hear a peep."

"You're just saying that to make me feel better."

Grant raised three fingers held close together. "No way. Scout's honor."

"You were a Boy Scout?"

"For about a week. Then came the flood."

"Your house was flooded?"

"No, the canyon about a mile from our town. We lived in Utah and horrendous spring rains sent a flash flood through the arroyos. The next day I went out to see the damage. The rush of water had sanded one of the walls down. The uncovered sedimentary layers were like a rainbow done in blacks, reds, and browns. I felt like I was standing in a time machine, looking at history.

"Then I saw something sticking out of the wall. It looked like a big sharpened stick. I took a rock from the stream bed and began to chip away the dirt around it. Soon I realized it was a tusk. My teenage mind imagined an entire mastodon behind it. In reality, it just turned out to be the tip of a tusk. But that thrill of discovery was enough. From then on, all I wanted to do was be a paleontologist."

"And how did you end up chasing live dinosaurs in Brazil?" Janaina said.

Grant thought his experience with the giant scorpions in the Montana cave system might be a little too much for Janaina to swallow. "That's a longer story for later. What set *you* on this path?"

"We have a dolphin native to our Amazonia rivers. You are familiar with this species?"

"It's pink, isn't it?"

"Yes and very rare. Many myths surround them. As a teenager, it, how you say, captured my soul. After completing university with a biology degree, I joined a group on a trip to clear one of its habitats of debris and old fishing lines. We traveled upriver for a few days, working along the shore each day and sleeping in our canoes at night.

"One night I awakened to a high-pitched scream, an awful chirping. The others still slept, so I paddled upstream under the moonlight to investigate. I rounded a bend to see a young dolphin beached on the riverbank. A great sore covered most of its head.

"Before I could paddle over to help it, a native Amazonian stepped out of the jungle. He wore practically nothing, just body paint and a headdress I couldn't even describe. He picked the dolphin up, gentle as a baby, and floated it out into the river. He massaged some kind of thick paste into the sore on the dolphin's head as he whispered something I couldn't understand to the dolphin. A minute later, the dolphin made a little splash, and he released it. It swam a circle in the river, and returned to blow a spray of water at the man who saved him."

"Wow," Grant said. "Amazing."

"Indeed it was. I realized that my quest to save the dolphin was too small. It wasn't just about the dolphin. It was about the river, and everything around it. Especially this native tribesman who could heal and communicate with the dolphin in a way I could only dream about. It all had to be protected, and if we protected the native tribes, they would protect the rest."

Grant ripped open a pack of crackers. "But to keep them in isolation from the present day seems a bit... I mean with all the advances we have, it seems callous."

"We can't add anything positive to their lives."

"But you saw that medicine. Maybe they can add to ours."

"At what cost? We may turn their culture into a present day cargo cult. At a minimum, we would introduce diseases. No peoples can be brought from pre-history into the 21st century unscathed. I'm content to learn through passive observation."

Grant smiled at her zeal. "Passive observation, passionate isolation."

"Exactly! We owe it to them to allow them to live their lives the way they have for thousands of years. You Americans have that attitude about wildlife. You set aside millions of acres for bison and antelope and bears to live free. Don't people deserve the same?"

"You have me convinced."

Janaina sighed. "Now I just need to convince a hundred million Brazilians and I win."

"I'm putting my money on you." Grant stuffed his trash back in the pouch. "Ready to solve all this place's mysteries?"

"Roger that!"

"What did you say?"

"It is a new American phrase I picked up from McCabe."

"Feel free to put that one back down."

They headed over to container where Katsoros and the security detail stood. As they arrived, McCabe sent Riffaud to "wake up the two geeks." Grant and Janaina took the soldier's place in the circle.

McCabe tossed his empty food pouch on the ground and flicked his little plastic spoon after it. He unfolded a photomosaic map and laid it on a box in front of the group. The highlands to the west were clear. McCabe pointed to a spot further east. "We're here."

Katsoros stepped up. "We'll start the search where the picture showed the apatosaurus." She pointed to a location near the plateau's eastern edge.

"Transworld Union will be preparing that rescue flight," McCabe said, "But their destination will be our intended landing site. We aren't near it and we don't have a way to tell them where we are." He pointed to the low clouds that covered the sky. "That perpetual low ceiling will make finding us tough."

"We'll need to make our location unmistakable from the air," Katsoros said. "And give the plane somewhere to land."

"I'll interrupt Griggs's beauty sleep and get him and the Bobcat on it," McCabe said.

"Should we try to rescue our pilots?" Janaina said.

"One of them is certainly dead," Grant said.

"And I wouldn't give the second one good odds of surviving that kind of impact," McCabe said.

"We have to focus on the mission with the limited time we have," Katsoros said.

"If you were the one in the plane, you'd think differently," Janaina said.

"But I'm not." Katsoros stuffed scraps of breakfast trash into the little plastic pouch. "Let's get moving."

Katsoros and McCabe stepped away with the map and a compass. Janaina balled her fists and stared after them.

"You two seem to get along well," Grant said.

"She tried to get me to stay back as an advisor instead of participating. She has something here to hide."

"Perhaps the dinosaurs?"

"Perhaps more than that."

Grant hoped not. Dinosaurs would be plenty.

***

Dixit went to work setting up his lab equipment and organizing some other larger boxes. Griggs set to work with the Bobcat stripping the charred trees from the clearing. Riffaud sat atop the container, sweating and watching for whatever this world was going to throw at them.

Hobart joined Grant, Janaina, and Katsoros on the trip to find the location from the photograph. Katsoros led the way, switching her focus from a compass to the map in her hand every minute or so. McCabe followed, rifle at the ready, in a non-stop scan of the jungle around them.

"Wow," Hobart said. "It will be so exciting to find scat."

"I say that every time I'm out for a walk," Grant said. He plucked up one of the leaves off a tree. "All these plants are... basic."

"How do you mean?" Janaina said.

"See how simplistic its structure is, the wider spacing between the sections of the leaf? It's all inefficient, unevolved. I've seen this species a hundred times, but only as fossils. Evolution took a pause up here a few million years ago. We are looking for dinosaurs, but the plant equivalent may be all around us."

About thirty minutes later, Katsoros froze. McCabe approached her and she whispered something to him. He moved back to the other three in the group.

"The spot from the photograph is just ahead. Just in case something's there, we'll go in slow and stay quiet."

Grant couldn't help but feel an upwelling of excitement. "Even if nothing's there, we should see evidence that something *was* there." He slapped Hobart on the shoulder. "Get the pooper scooper ready."

Hobart didn't smile.

The group followed Katsoros, slow as a procession at Sunday Mass. They broke out into a small, grassy clearing. The far side stopped at the plateau's edge and gave a clear view of the cloud cover over the land below.

On the ground in the center of the clearing lay the neck and head of an apatosaurus.

Or at least a crude approximation of one. Hand-carved from solid wood, it appeared to have started life as the trunk and branch of a tree. The totem matched the head from the photograph perfectly in shape, though the long distance photo had masked its lack of detail and uneven surface. The head's only defining feature was a single groove around the middle. The toppled totem had broken away from a rotted base.

"Mystery solved," Katsoros said.

Grant sagged with disappointment at the hoax. Janaina rushed to it with a shout of joy.

"Look at this!" She practically cooed it as she ran her fingertips along the crosshatched pattern etched on the creature's neck.

"My nephew whittles better-looking things than that," McCabe said.

"I'm sure he does. With a knife. Look at the pattern of the cuts. This was shaped with stone."

"A local tribe?" Grant asked.

"And an isolated one. Metal blades from the developed world are always an early bit of assimilation for these isolated groups. Whoever carved this had none."

McCabe walked off and started to examine the clearing's perimeter.

Katsoros face went red. "Dammit, how could there be people up here? There's no other animal life."

"That would be a good question," Grant said. "And why would they carve something like that?"

Janaina wasn't listening. She started a slow survey of the area around the carving. She stopped and scooped up a second totem buried in the grass. This one was clearly older, more weathered and riven with cracks. Grant walked over and inadvertently stepped on another. It disintegrated into powder on contact.

"They've been doing this for a long time," Janaina said. "Keeping this place clear and making these carvings. In your Pacific Northwest, the animals on a totem aren't representing animals, but attributes, or sometimes a tribal clan. Perhaps that's what these represent."

McCabe returned. "Whoever put it up here isn't here often. There aren't any worn footpaths through the jungle coming to this spot. And that thing was put up a long time ago."

"These would have taken many months to make with stone tools." Janaina returned to the newest totem and gave it a closer inspection. "This wood is from a walking palm. That's how it got that graceful curve. That grows in the rainforest where it floods, not up here with these plants from the past. This came from the river valley."

She marched to the edge of the clearing. It ended in a cliff. She went to her hands and knees and peered over the edge.

"Well, look what we have here," she said.

The others joined her. Up the cliff face ran a series of crudely carved hand holds. Between some, mahogany stakes protruded from crevices in the rock.

"Someone climbed up here?" Katsoros said. "Carrying those things?"

"It looks that way. I've done a lot of climbing, some of it free climbing. Those little divots in the stone are the right spacing for someone a bit shorter than we are."

Grant wanted to add the climbers were also a lot stronger.

Hobart stepped to the edge, and looked down. He swooned a bit and his face went pale. He took two steps back. "Heights aren't my thing."

"Heights are fine," Grant said, taking a step back himself. "It's falling off them that doesn't appeal to me."

"The clearing faces east," Janaina said, "so I'd guess they come here yearly, tied to the solar cycle, like Aztec and Mayan rituals." She sat back from the edge and stared into the jungle. "The tribes have many stories they pass down through the generations. Oral tradition is all they have. One is about monsters in the clouds, living in the violent world from which all things were born, a gateway to the chaos before the gods imposed order through man. The stories were believed to be allegorical, like Mount Olympus to the Greeks. Perhaps they have more basis in fact than we believed."

"And these totems?"

"Are supposed to keep everything up here," Janaina looked over the cliff, "from going down there."

"More superstitious crap," McCabe said. "I've been all over. Everyone has their ghost stories. None of them are true. The more backward the group, the more BS they believe."

"You can't just discount native traditions," Janaina said.

"Sure I can. We've spent almost a day here. Haven't seen any monsters, haven't even seen traces of any monsters. I'm going to go with there being no monsters. Not to say there might not be dangers, like jaguars and anacondas, but I'm taking dinosaurs off my worry list."

"Agreed," Katsoros said. "Let's head back."

McCabe led the way this time, his weapon held much more casually, his pace much quicker. Hobart looked downright disappointed. Katsoros, the opposite, which Grant thought odd since she and Transworld Union had organized the whole expedition around the dinosaurs' existence.

"Sorry it appears we are without dinosaurs," Janaina said to Grant about half way back to camp. "You made the trip for nothing."

"It was a long shot," Grant said. "Sorry we didn't discover any isolated tribes up here. You also made your trip for nothing."

"Not at all. I found out there's a tribe down there in the valley. One with a pretty rich belief in monsters in the clouds. I have enough evidence to get the right people interested in doing area observations."

Hobart plucked a leaf from a passing tree. "And if these species are new to science, there's still some new genetic material to bring back and study. Not as exciting as a dinosaur, but you never know what it will lead to."

Collecting plant specimens wasn't the most exciting way to kill the time before extraction, but Grant figured it beat doing nothing.

When they returned to the camp, Riffaud had set up the solar panels. Griggs had made some progress knocking down and removing the trees left standing in the burn area. He'd started a decent pile of trunks at the area's edge. Dixit had set up his mobile lab under the parachute near the container. A laptop and some analyzing equipment sat on a folding table. A stack of boxes made a wall behind him. He seemed busy for a guy without any DNA samples to process. Katsoros broke from the group and went to Dixit.

McCabe called Riffaud and Griggs in to brief them on what they'd found.

"Can I buy you lunch?" Grant asked Janaina. "I know a place that serves a great pouch."

"Can we get a table without a reservation?"

"I have some pull with the staff."

She smiled and they walked over to the open box of military rations in the supply stacks. She pulled out two.

"Pick your poison," she said.

Grant took the bag on the right.

"Now see," Janaina said. "I got that phrase right, and it makes no sense at all. Why offer someone poison?"

CHAPTER NINE

While the group ate lunch, Katsoros did a rapid, increasingly irritated search of the supplies they'd parachuted in from the aircraft. She grimaced and slammed closed the lid of the last crate. A few minutes later, she called the group together beside the sleeping container. She'd stuck the map to the container wall. She looked worried.

"We just finished inventory," Katsoros said. "The situation is we have most of what we packed for the mission. But I think we need some insurance that the rescue flight will find us. We need to find the crash site and find a radio."

"Yesterday that was a bad idea," Grant said.

"No, looking for dead bodies was a bad idea," Katsoros said. "Salvaging a working radio might save our lives. Plus, there might be first aid kits, who knows what."

McCabe stepped up and pointed to a section of the map. "We are right here." He pointed to another spot on the map. "Based on Dino Doc's description and the smoke I saw, the plane is likely somewhere here." McCabe circled an area on the map to the northwest. "This flatter ground here? That's where they'd try to put down the damaged plane."

"How far is that?" Katsoros said.

"A few klicks. Depending on the terrain and the jungle, at least two hours out and two back."

"Then we'd best get moving," Katsoros said. "I want us all back in the box before sunset." She turned to Grant and Janaina. "You two are with us."

"Dixit shouldn't miss this fun," Grant said. "Let me be the one to tell him."

"I'll take care of that. You two pack water for the trip." Katsoros headed off in Dixit's direction.

"I really wanted to tell that weaselly lab rat he needed to trek through the jungle," Grant said.

"Is that an American thing?" Janaina said. "Mixing your animal descriptors like that?"

"He deserved both references. Who am I to deny him his due?"

Katsoros passed by with Hobart in tow. "Mr. Hobart will be accompanying us to retrieve any samples the group might come across, instead of Dr. Dixit."

Once she was out of earshot, Grant said, "That seals the deal. Dixit is a cowardly jackass."

"And there's your third animal descriptor," Janaina said. "I'm beginning to second guess buying your book when we get back."

Grant ignored the barb. "I could accept Dixit not going with us to the sacrifice area, so he could set up his gear. But this is a long hike, and we are likely to find signs of dinosaurs if there are any out there to find. Scientific curiosity alone should compel him to go."

"You are taking this personally for some reason."

"That kid Hobart's in over his head. And I've seen too many overworked assistants. Hell, I *was* one. Hate to see them taken advantage of."

"Don't let your reaction keep you, and the rest of us, from getting the job done."

Janaina walked off. Grant mulled her warning, then dismissed it.

***

Half an hour later, Katsoros again took the lead as the group headed out into the jungle. McCabe followed with a wary eye on the rainforest around them. Hobart bumbled along in the center with a wad of sample bags in his backpack. Grant and Janaina took up the rear.

The high canopy blocked most daylight and left the ground clear enough that they didn't have to bushwhack their way through like Grant had from the Bobcat crash site. That was a blessing but the twilight lighting didn't put Grant at ease.

"Still no dinosaurs yet," Janaina said. "Disappointed?"

"The scientist is disappointed," Grant said. "The man is thrilled that nothing has tried to eat us. Anything make you think any people have been here other than at that sacrifice site?"

"No, but we likely wouldn't see anything. The local tribes, how you say, leave a light footprint. Here the double meaning for 'footprint' is true. You have to stumble into a village to find them."

Grant wanted to keep their conversation going. He found the jungle's silence unnerving. Considering that they were here in search of wildlife, it was bizarre that they hadn't been entertained by any birdsong, or been annoyed by the buzz of flying bugs. He'd been to desert excavation sites with more animals.

Just over two hours into the trip, a sharp smell like kerosene filled the air. The unnatural scent cut through the earthy jungle aroma like a knife.

"Ugh, what is that?" Janaina said.

"Aviation fuel," McCabe said. "We're close."

He checked the direction of the breeze and angled the group off to the right. Soon the charcoal-scent of burned wood joined the kerosene's tang. Ash coated the earth where the ground cover had burned away in a flash fire. Ahead lay the wreckage of their plane.

The pilot might have put the aircraft down on flat ground, but it hadn't made a difference. The plane had plunged through the jungle canopy at a low angle and shaved away treetops on the way down. The wings had snapped off and lay twisted at each side of the crash scene. The fuselage lay further ahead, nose half-buried in the dirt, tail stabilizers sheared off and missing. The rear cargo ramp was gone and the tail of the aircraft faced them like the opening to a cave.

"Even if the pilot survived," Grant said, "the bird strike definitely killed the copilot. His corpse will still be in the cockpit."

"I'll check it out up front," McCabe said, "and grab the radio. All of you scour the rest of the plane for anything useful."

McCabe shouldered his rifle and led the group to the plane. The repulsive stench of death grew as they got closer, as if exhaled from the wreck's dark, open maw.

They stepped inside and McCabe went to the cockpit. Katsoros began to search through containers jumbled against the left bulkhead. A red-and-white first aid kit hung on the right bulkhead. A slash across the center exposed puffy white insulation. Janaina popped it off the wall pins and unzipped it for inspection. Hobart paused outside the plane, seemingly entranced by the jungle around him.

Grant made his way to the cockpit. Whether out of respect for the pilot who gave them all a chance to bail out, or whether by some need for personal closure, he wasn't sure.

McCabe stood behind the copilot's seat. The shattered windshield left the cockpit open to the outside. The place was a shambles, with dials and control switches missing, navigation manuals shredded and strewn about.

The copilot was there as Grant remembered him, decapitated, but the body was bloodier and more bloated than before. He hoped the captain had survived and made it out alive, but a glance to the right dashed those hopes. The pilot's body sat in the chair, still strapped in, both hands still at the controls.

"You said there was a bird strike?" McCabe said.

Grant pointed at the shattered left cockpit window. "Right through there."

McCabe scooped an animal off the ground. "What kind of a bird do you call this?"

With a grip on each wing he spread the creature out in front of Grant. Leathery skin covered bat-like wings that spread almost a meter wide. Two short, muscular legs hung down from its rectangular body. A long, pointed bill stuck out in front and a crest that nearly duplicated it ran along the back of its head.

Grant couldn't hide his excitement. "That is a pterosaur."

Katsoros stepped up behind him. "A what?"

"A flying reptile from the Cretaceous period," Grant said. "Extinct. Until now."

Grant reached out to touch it. McCabe tossed it at him in frustration. Grant caught it under the wings with both hands.

"You mean the plane was downed by these little flying dinosaurs?"

"They're carnivores, likely pack hunters. The big lumbering plane probably looked like an easy meal. They'd never seen one before."

Grant examined the pterosaur in detail, amazed to be holding this link to an era millions of years ago, somehow completely glossing over the fact that it almost got him killed.

"Damn," Katsoros said. She sounded more annoyed than stunned. "Hobart! Get in here for some samples."

Thudding footsteps along the aircraft floor announced Hobart's approach. He stuck his head in the cabin. "You found something?"

Grant smiled. "It isn't poo, but maybe you can do something with it."

Grant held out the dead pterosaur. Hobart made a girlish shriek and shied away.

"But dinosaur feces, that's okay?" Grant said.

"No, I'm fine, you just startled me, that's all." Hobart took a deep breath, as if summoning some composure. He put on a latex glove, grabbed the pterosaur by the neck, and then retreated to the rear of the aircraft.

"So psyched he's on our team," Grant said.

"Funny, that's what I said about you," McCabe said.

Grant stepped out of the cockpit to avoid escalating the verbal battle. He hopped out of the back of the plane. Janaina dropped down beside him.

"*Ai, meu Deus!* That was an actual dinosaur, wasn't it?"

"As near as I can tell."

"I have to admit, I thought finding dinosaurs was fantasy nonsense."

"After the disappointment at the sacrifice site, a pterosaur is more than I expected. I'm daring to hope we may even see an actual apatosaurus."

"Can we encounter that one without it trying to kill us?"

"It's an herbivore. The odds are in our favor."

Katsoros joined them with a dark canvas messenger bag slung across her chest.

"You trampled through the jungle for a bag?" Janaina said.

"It has all the expedition records and permits."

"Super duper," Grant said. "We need something to get the night's fire going."

Katsoros's face went red in anger. "Why don't you add some value here and tell me about these birds that crashed the plane."

"Flying reptiles. The accepted theory is that that they flocked like birds, hunted in a swarm."

"So are they going to swoop out of the trees on us on the way back?"

"No, they don't do trees. They don't have perching feet like a bird. They have lizard feet. They likely walked along the ground on all fours, wings swept back and up. Likely lived in burrows or between rocks."

"So how did they fly?" Janaina asked.

"The theory is they climbed up to a high point and jumped."

"In a group, and then took down airplanes?" Katsoros said.

"It does look like that theory may need to be revised," Grant said.

CHAPTER TEN

McCabe jumped out of the back of the aircraft and landed beside the group. He held a radio he'd pulled from the console between the cockpit seats. One of the pilot's headsets hung around his neck. "I can rig this up. It won't broadcast all the way back to São Paulo, but it'll reach the rescue plane when it gets here. I'll make damn sure they find us."

"We don't want to miss that ride," Katsoros said.

"We need to get away from this plane." McCabe looked at the sinking sun. "Those bodies are an easy food source and I don't want to find out what kind of nocturnal creatures they attract."

Katsoros pulled out the map. "We walked in an arc to get here. We can get back quicker in a straight line."

McCabe looked over her shoulder. "Terrain looks rougher, but it might be faster if we hump it. Shoot an azimuth and let's do it." He handed the radio to Janaina. "Here you go."

Janaina took the radio. She underestimated the weight and almost dropped it. "How did I get to carry this?"

"Because I'm carrying this." McCabe unslung the rifle from his shoulder.

Janaina stuffed the radio into her backpack.

Grant suddenly felt defenseless. Carnivorous dinosaurs stalked the jungle. He climbed back into the plane in search of a weapon. He grabbed a small red crash ax from the bulkhead under where Janaina had removed the first aid kit. It didn't have weight or range, but the pterosaurs were relatively small.

The broken remnant of one of the struts from the missing cargo door hung from the bulkhead. Grant slipped the ax into his belt, grabbed the strut with both hands, and pulled. The shattered mounting bracket squealed and then snapped with a crack. The steel shaft stretched a bit longer than a baseball bat and felt twice as heavy.

"Batter up, pterosaur," he said to himself.

He realized the irony of discovering an amazing extinct species, then minutes later trying to figure out a way to kill the first one that approached him. He looked around and didn't find anything else that might be of defensive value. He jumped back out of the plane and handed the ax to Janaina.

"Just in case," he said.

"I will wish only to use it for making firewood," Janaina said. She slipped it into her belt.

Hobart returned with the pterosaur sealed in a big Ziploc bag. He slid it into his backpack. "Any other samples in the cockpit?"

"Bits and pieces," Katsoros said. "Likely contaminated with human DNA. You have the best of them."

McCabe checked his watch. "Let's roll."

Katsoros took out her compass and sighted a tree along the return azimuth. "Ready." She set out for the edge of the crash site. The others followed.

***

The route back to the camp may have been more direct, but it proved far less passable. The ground rose and fell like waves in a rough sea. The jungle was far denser, a sea of waist-high ferns under a low canopy of close-packed palms. Thorn-like spikes coated the palms' lower trunks. The group left an open trail of crushed ferns behind them. With any breeze blocked, the air enveloped Grant in a thick, humid blanket. In minutes, sweat drenched him.

The group walked in silence with Katsoros and her compass in the lead. She stopped every few hundred steps to check their course.

McCabe had remained on high alert, his finger never off his rifle's trigger guard. Hobart kept cringing and adjusting the straps of his pack against the weight or the pterosaur. Ziploc bag or not, Grant swore he could smell the stink of the thing as he followed in Hobart's wake.

Ferns rustled off to the right. Grant spun to look that way, but everything was still.

Ferns rustled again, this time to the left. Louder.

"Did you hear that?" Janaina said.

"I wish I hadn't," Grant answered.

Behind and to the left, what looked like a reddish shark fin broke above the tops of the ferns. A second one appeared a quarter meter beside it. In tandem, they alternated in a little forward-pause-forward dance in parallel with the group's path. Ferns snapped in sync with the motion.

"There's something out there." Hobart practically shrieked the warning.

Two more fins surfaced to the right. Then another set.

"Let's go," McCabe said. "Double-time it!"

Katsoros broke into a jog. McCabe took the rear as everyone tried to keep up with Katsoros. He leveled his rifle at the ocean of ferns behind them. Two more sets of fins rose on the left.

McCabe paused and aimed. He fired and the rifle's three-round burst echoed between the trees. Bullets clipped fern tops like an invisible scythe. A high-pitched shriek pierced the air and an explosion of blood blossomed above the ferns. The fins disintegrated.

A sharp, hawk-like scream sounded from the other sets of fins. They tore through the ferns, zeroing in on the group.

Grant's heart pounded hard. He gripped the door strut so tightly that his hands turned white. Katsoros sprinted and he struggled to keep up.

Behind them, a set of fins broke through onto the group's trodden path. It was a pterosaur, charging on all fours, wings tucked up in the air creating the illusion of fins. Its head swept back at an almost impossible angle, bill pointing straight out like a jousting knight's lance, head crest tucked between its pumping wings. Eyes burned a fiery red on each side of the bill, laser-locked on the retreating humans.

McCabe fired behind him as he ran. The rounds clipped one wing and shattered the top joint. The pterosaur wailed and collapsed to that side and spun into the ferns.

The other pterosaurs leapt into the air. The jungle was too confined for flight, but each managed a single, accelerative beat of its wings toward the group. Two dove on Janaina, attacking from both sides. The third made a beeline for Katsoros.

The weight of the pterosaurs drove Janaina screaming to the ground. Hobart tripped and fell face first into the ferns. The other pterosaur clamped its leg talons on the crown of Katsoros' head. With a snap of its head it drove its bill into her left shoulder.

Another pterosaur burst from the ferns behind them. With two flaps of its wings, it rose to the canopy, then dove for McCabe with an ear-splitting shriek of fury.

McCabe snapped his rifle to his shoulder and fired. The pterosaur exploded in a cloud of red mist. Its wings continued forwards and dropped at either side of his feet.

Katsoros dropped to her knees with a panicked wail. She grabbed the pterosaur legs where the talons gripped her skull. She pulled but they didn't budge.

McCabe ran to Katsoros. He raised the rifle and drove the butt against the pterosaur's head. Its bill shattered as its neck snapped. The dinosaur went limp and toppled into the ferns.

Grant skidded to a stop beside Janaina. Screaming, face down on the ground, she'd covered her head with her arms. The two pterosaurs gripped her backpack as they pecked at her shoulders.

Grant aimed the jagged end of the strut at one pterosaur and plunged it into its body. The shaft pierced the creature's skin with the sound of tearing leather. Blood gushed from the wound. The pterosaur let loose and sprang from Janaina's back. It scampered away through the ferns.

The second pterosaur swept back one wing and struck Grant square in the face. His glasses sliced a gash in the bridge of his nose and everything went white. He stumbled backwards and dropped on his butt. The pterosaur ripped Janaina's pack from her back and darted into the tiny forest of ferns. The dragged backpack left a flattened trail.

Grant rolled Janaina over. She shook like she was being electrocuted. Her eyes were wide with panic. Grant shook her by the shoulders.

"Janaina! They're gone. It's okay now." He looked Janaina's quivering body over. "Are you hurt?"

Janaina seemed to pause to do a mental self-diagnostic. "No... I'm... I'm okay."

Next to them, Hobart rolled up from the ferns, looking dazed.

McCabe dropped the magazine from his rifle, counted the rounds, and slapped it back into place. He looked down at Hobart then went over to Katsoros. He winced as he inspected the tip of the bill that protruded from her shoulder. Katsoros pressed her hands against her wounded head as blood seeped between her fingers.

"Oh my God... oh my God... oh my God," she whispered to herself.

McCabe knelt beside her and checked the stub of the bill in her shoulder.

"That's not in deep," he said.

"Could have fooled me," she said.

"Christ knows where that thing has been," he said. "I'm going to pull it out to minimize the chance for infection."

Katsoros sighed and closed her eyes. "Okay. Let me—"

Lightning fast, McCabe gripped her shoulder with his left hand and yanked the bill out with his right. Katsoros bit back a scream.

"All done," he said. He pulled a medical compress pack from his cargo pants and tore open the plastic pouch. He unfolded it and pressed it against her wound from under her shirt. "Keep the pressure on there until it stops bleeding. We'll clean it up good when we get back to camp."

McCabe made a sling for Katsoros's arm from her scarf.

"What kind of bird attacks from the ground like that?" Hobart said.

"One that was still half-terrestrial," Grant answered. "Pterosaurs are an evolutionary step toward birds. In the confines of the jungle floor, they switched tactics. Scientists theorized about this ability based on the musculature. I'd be excited about the discovery if it hadn't turned into a near-fatal experience."

"They'll keep hunting us?" Hobart said.

"They weren't hunting," Janaina said. "If they were hunting us, they would have outnumbered us by more, made the odds of success overwhelming. That's what animals do."

"Then why did they attack us?" Hobart said.

"They didn't," Grant said. "They attacked Janaina. And they jumped Ms. Katsoros to get her to stop and make Janaina a better target."

"Me?" Janaina said.

"They wanted that backpack. As soon as they had it, mission over. And the only thing they saw you put in it was the radio."

"So they attacked to reclaim the radio?" McCabe said. "Birds don't know how radios work."

"Again, they aren't birds."

"But they are close relatives," Janaina said. "They wanted it for some reason. And crows demonstrate similar cooperation and sense of community."

"Those pterosaurs have three times the brain of a crow," Grant added.

"So they have what they want," Hobart said, "and won't attack us again on the way back to camp?"

"I'd guess they won't," Grant said.

He didn't want to worry Hobart more by adding that there was likely some other creature ready to assume the pterosaur's place as a predator.

CHAPTER ELEVEN

Grant sighed with relief when they finally broke out of the jungle and into the clearing where they'd set up camp. A break in the clouds delivered bright sunlight and a light breeze swept down from the western highlands. It felt like being reborn.

Griggs had been hard at work with the Bobcat. He'd lengthened the clearing and it had started to resemble a landing strip. Downed tree trunks lined the sides like a giant had emptied a box of enormous toothpicks. But it wasn't anywhere near as long as the runway they'd taken off from in São Paulo. Grant wondered how long it would have to be.

Riffaud stood atop the shipping container. He waved the group in and shouted across the clearing to Griggs on the Bobcat. Griggs stopped pushing over a tree and drove back over to the container.

As the group approached the container, Dixit wandered around from behind it.

"Did you find the plane?" he asked.

"Yes, and pterosaurs," Katsoros said.

Dixit's eyes widened with surprise.

"But the radio didn't make it back with us," Katsoros said.

Dixit's face fell. Katsoros raised the messenger bag up with her good arm and smiled. "But I did find this."

Dixit looked immensely relieved. "That is certainly a good thing."

"Absolutely," Grant deadpanned. "Having all our paperwork in order makes all the difference in the world."

Dixit turned and Katsoros followed him back to his makeshift lab area.

"And Hobart's okay," Grant called after them. He turned to Hobart. "Dixit looked pretty worried about you, didn't he?"

"Dr. Dixit has a lot of responsibility." Hobart headed off to follow Dixit.

Griggs stepped up beside McCabe. Riffaud hopped down from the container and joined them. He pointed to Katsoros. "What happened to her?"

"We got ambushed," McCabe said. "Same birds that brought down the plane."

"Pterosaurs, actually," Grant offered.

McCabe shot him a dirty look. "Half-bat, half-lizard, all deadly. Griggs, I need you to redirect your work to making a defensive berm around this location. If they come at us on the ground, I want high points where I can mow them down with clean fields of fire. Riffaud, the bastards fly, so keep your eyes on the sky. The sons of bitches can probably punch through the steel container with their bills."

Grant doubted they could, but an hour ago he didn't even know they were alive, so he wasn't going to offer an opinion likely to turn out being wrong.

"We'll need to refill the water containers," Riffaud said.

"There's a stream at the north edge of the airstrip," McCabe said. "Dino Doc, think you can handle that?"

"Finally," Grant said. "My dream of becoming a pack mule is fulfilled."

"Two sterilization tablets in every container, smart ass. Unless another of your dreams is spending hours squatting over a dirt hole."

"It's like you've been reading my bucket list."

McCabe was about to retort and stopped short. Instead he pointed to the water cans. "Get to it before it gets dark."

Grant grabbed an empty five-gallon jerry can in each hand and headed to the north end of the "airstrip." Griggs might have been an amazing soldier, but he left a lot to be desired as a heavy equipment operator. The ground was still uneven and plenty of low stumps jutted from the field. He hoped Griggs knew what clearance the aircraft needed.

At the clearing's edge, a stream ran into the jungle. The water ran fast and crystal clear, about three feet deep. He unscrewed the tops, dropped two tablets into each can, and waded into the water. It felt refreshing. He submerged both cans in the stream. Water filled both in an instant. He tried to pull them out of the stream.

They didn't move.

He grabbed one with both hands and yanked. It felt like it weighed fifty pounds. He did the math and realized that was damn near what it did weigh. On all his paleontology field excursions, he'd always had interns who did this kind of heavy lifting. He pulled the first container up and out of the stream, then the second. He screwed the tops back on and took a deep breath to prepare for the trip back to camp.

Something along the clearing's edge caught his eye. The ground had been dug up, but not in a pattern the Bobcat would have created. Something almost glowed in the dirt at the bottom of the hole.

Grant stepped over to the two-meter divot. The ground had indeed been excavated about a half meter down, then the pit was lined with small sticks and leaves. Under an impression of Bobcat treads lay smashed eggshells, the contents dried and splattered. He picked up a piece. The eggs had been large. He put it in his pocket.

Grant checked the jungle by the nest. There were some small bushes at the edges, and the trees had deep gashes across the trunks about waist high. The grass had been pounded flat. Uprooted trees lay scattered around the edge. Something had cleared the area before digging that nest.

This did not look good. A large animal had made that nest, and Griggs had turned it into scrambled eggs. In an ecosystem this isolated, a loss like that might be species-catastrophic.

He stomped back to the jerry cans and without thinking tried to yank them off the ground. Pain raced up through both shoulders and met at his neck. He dropped the cans.

He picked them back up slowly, and began the trek back to camp.

Multiple stops later, he trudged back into camp. McCabe met him, smiling.

"Those are a little heavier full, aren't they?"

"I hardly noticed."

McCabe walked off still grinning. Janaina approached Grant.

"Hauling fresh water home," she said. "Welcome to the Amazonia lifestyle."

"A month after we get back," Grant said, "there will be three Starbucks here. But I did find something other than fresh water."

He pulled an eggshell from his pocket and handed it to her.

"Hatched eggs?" she said.

"Crushed eggs. Griggs ran over some kind of nest with the Bobcat."

"A pterosaur nest?"

"Based on the size of those adult pterosaurs? No. This nest was for something much bigger, not the kind of mother I want us to have pissed off."

"Something dangerous?"

"We just killed its brood. That automatically makes it dangerous."

***

As daylight disappeared, Griggs stopped work to let the Bobcat recharge while the solar panels still hummed. A five-foot berm encircled the camp and most of it had a tangle of trees along the top.

Grant sat in the dirt, back against the warm side of the shipping container they all called home. The setting sun had switched the air temperature from "broil" to simply "uncomfortable," but the temperature differential had spawned a breeze that made it seem more bearable.

Janaina stepped around the corner of the container with two pouches of dehydrated meals in her hands. "Ready for dinner?"

"As long I don't have to dress. I left my tuxedo back in the plane."

"You are okay. Dress code is jungle-crash-casual." She handed him a meal and sat beside him.

"Don't be too loud," Grant said. "Riffaud is sleeping in the container so he can cover night shift."

"In this heat?"

"Yeah. Those three guys are tough."

"Are you worried about a pterosaur night attack?"

"Not really. The pterosaurs are diurnal, day fliers, poor night vision, cold blooded. They'll sleep all night, then rise when the sun is up to help keep them warm."

"You're just saying that to make me feel safer."

"No, I'm saying it make me feel safer."

"Is it working?"

"One hundred percent."

Janaina knit her brows. "That is your sarcasm voice, yes?"

"Yes, it is. How do you like it?"

"It takes some getting used to."

"My ex-wife would agree."

CHAPTER TWELVE

Grant and the others slept through the night without interruption. He awakened half-thrilled and half-surprised that his prediction of the pterosaurs' sleep pattern was correct. He was the last one to rise. Sunlight streamed through the container's open door.

"I can sleep, sitting up, in daylight, in suffocating humidity," he said to himself. "I can sleep anywhere."

He pulled his glasses from his pocket, unstrapped himself, and headed outside. The temperature was cooler and the humidity had abated. Janaina smiled and approached him.

"Nice of you to finally get up."

"I left a wakeup call, but the front desk clerk is useless. I'd hate to oversleep and miss the fifteen livable minutes we have outside."

"This is much better than at the plateau's base down by the river. I thought you were used to doing dinosaur digs all summer?"

"In the desert."

"You will adapt. Eventually."

"Or sweat to death trying. Where's the Transworld contingent?"

"Katsoros and Dixit were already playing with his toys when I woke up. And they don't want me anywhere near the equipment."

"Dixit gets friendlier every day. When we get back he and I are going for an English pub crawl."

"And then you can go to a soccer match." Janaina smiled. "See, I am catching your sarcasm voice."

"And where's Hobart?"

"Over there cleaning up."

Near the far side of the encircling berm, Hobart stood shirtless by one of the five gallon cans Grant had dragged back from the stream. Soap suds enveloped his head and hands.

"He's making the next water run," Grant said.

McCabe and Riffaud stood beside a waist-high pile of boxes. The satellite phone sat on top. McCabe poked at it with a tiny screwdriver, cursed, and slammed the screwdriver down.

Something rustled in the brush on the other side of the berm. Janaina spun in that direction.

"Did you hear that?"

She and Grant climbed halfway up the berm and peered over the top.

A furry creature the size of a medium dog burst out of the woods and charged toward them. The body looked like a guinea pig, but with longer legs. However, the face was decidedly narrower and far more rat-like. It sprinted fast as a greyhound.

"Hell, no," Grant said. He and Janaina scrambled down the berm. "McCabe!"

Hobart was walking from the wash area drying the inside of his ears with a towel. Grant's cry for McCabe drew Dixit and Katsoros. They stepped around to the front of the container with looks of confusion.

McCabe and Riffaud snapped to alert, weapons at their shoulders, aimed over Grant's head at the top of the berm.

The animal crested the berm at a sprint, teeth bared.

Both men fired almost at once. One bullet kicked up a spray of dirt at the animal's feet, but the second round caught it in the shoulder. The creature squealed as the impact knocked it to the ground.

The top of the berm exploded. A swarm of the animals crested it like a brown, furry wave. Not in a directed attack on the Transworld team, but in a chaotic, frenzied rush to the west.

Grant and Janaina made a beeline for the stack of supplies. Grant scaled the pile, then pulled Janaina up after him. The creatures washed past them like a surging sea. Grant choked on their ripe, musky stench.

Katsoros and Dixit jumped into the container and shut the door. McCabe scrambled to the container's roof and Riffaud took a position at the door.

Hobart hesitated, stepped to join Grant and Janaina on the pallet, hesitated, and then turned to run to the container.

The pause was his undoing.

The herd bowled him over. With a scream, he disappeared under a cloud of dust and an undulating sea of fur.

The two soldiers opened fire. Three-round bursts peppered the horde and sent up sprays of blood and entrails. But the surge didn't slacken. Whatever the creatures were running from was far scarier than the introduction of gunpowder and flying lead. They rushed past the container. Dixit's equipment toppled to the ground.

Then from the jungle sounded a branch-snapping crash too large for the swarm to have made. A chorus of squeals followed. Then another crash.

The last of the swarm passed over the western berm. The herd thundered toward Griggs in the Bobcat. He jerked the machine to a stop and gawked as they churned up an ashy dust cloud all around him. The creatures disappeared into the jungle on the west side.

"Are you okay?" Grant asked Janaina.

"A little twist to my ankle, but nothing permanent." She climbed down from the containers.

Grant hopped down. They both went over to Hobart. He sat up in a daze, hair askew. The creatures had ripped a gash in his left leg. Grant reached down and helped him up.

"W-what were those things?" Hobart said.

"As near as I can make out, something close to a phoberomys," Grant said. "An extinct species of giant, well, guinea pigs. Their fossils were discovered about thirty years ago. But these have developed a much leaner face."

"And sharp teeth," Hobart said. He winced as shifted the weight off his bleeding leg.

"Let's get that cleaned and covered," Janaina said. She draped his arm across her shoulder and helped him hop over to one of the boxes marked with a red cross.

Katsoros stuck her head out of the container. Then Dixit burst past her and went straight for his equipment. He cursed, dropped to his knees, and began to right the toppled computers and scanners. Grant stepped over to give him a hand. He lifted an open laptop from the ground. Dixit's eyes widened.

"Please do not assist me," Dixit said. "I can take care of this. It is very specialized."

Grant bristled at being treated like a flailing child around fine china. "I've spent a lot of time in the field and in labs working with equipment like this."

"I am certain not equipment like this," Dixit said. He pulled the laptop from Grant's hand. "I would greatly appreciate you keeping a distance."

Grant raised his hands in surrender. "Fine, fine. I'll let you play with all your own toys."

McCabe hopped down from the top of the container. "Whatever those things were, they're deep into the jungle on the other side now."

"They weren't attacking us," Grant said. "They're herbivorous."

"Not worried about them," McCabe said. "Worried about what was chasing them."

He shouted to Griggs to get back to clearing the field. Griggs acknowledged with a wave and restarted the Bobcat.

McCabe pointed at Riffaud. "Take a position on the container. I want a warning if anything else comes charging out of the jungle." He poked Grant in the chest with his index finger. "You're coming with me to find that 'anything else'."

That "anything else" had sounded pretty damn big to Grant.

"I'm more an extinct animal kind of guy," Grant said. "Dixit's your man for this."

McCabe slapped him on the shoulder. "You write monster fiction. It's time you lived it."

If only McCabe knew that Grant had lived plenty of it in the Montana caverns.

Hobart limped past them to Dixit. The lower half of one pant leg was cut away and exposed a wrap of blood-stippled bandages where he'd been injured. He carried a dead phoberomys in his blue-gloved hands. A bullet had turned its head to hamburger. Hobart stood before Dixit looking like a dog awaiting reinforcement for fetching a ball.

"Please do not bring the carcass here," Dixit said. He laid two wrapped syringes on top of the dead animal and then gave Hobart a shooing motion with his hands. "Samples. Bring me samples."

Cowardly Dixit wasn't going to volunteer for McCabe's monster search, so either Hobart or Grant would need to go. Grant wasn't keen about it, but he wasn't about to try pushing the responsibility off on limping Hobart.

McCabe nudged Grant toward the berm. Less than a threat, but more than a request. McCabe's tight smile promised it could easily become more of the former. Grant started a slow climb up the berm. He paused at the top and checked the area between the berm and the jungle. Open and quiet. The mini-horde had churned up a trail across the clearing.

McCabe drew his machete from his belt and offered it to Grant. "Here, a little self-defense."

"Very little."

"All you'll need when I'm your first line."

McCabe hopped down off the berm and began to backtrack the phoberomys horde's trail. Grant looked at the machete in his hand and felt uncomfortably like a kid playing pirate. He followed McCabe in.

It didn't take long to find where the other creature had attacked the phoberomys pack. A swath of ground level jungle had been trampled flat. Uprooted plants lay along the perimeter like felled soldiers after battle. Blood splatted some of the leaves. Two phoberomys heads lay on the ground.

"Something this big wasn't feeding," Grant said. "It was just snacking."

McCabe looked at the trunk of one of the trees. Deep, waist-high gouges exposed white, pulpy bark. "And it eats trees."

Grant ran a finger through the gash. "This wasn't done by teeth. Some kind of horn or spike grazed it." He checked the ground around the tree. A few big palm leaves lay crushed. He swept them aside and revealed a deep footprint in the soft ground, almost a meter wide with three broad toes.

"What the hell made that?" McCabe said.

"First guess?" Grant said. "A dinosaur."

And from the look of the familiar, slashed damage to the trees, the same kind that just lost a nest of eggs.

CHAPTER THIRTEEN

As soon as Grant and McCabe returned to the campsite, McCabe went to brief Riffaud. Griggs and the Bobcat were back to clearing the future runway.

The others gathered around Grant and he told them about the site they'd found in the jungle.

"Looks like we have a whole new dinosaur," Katsoros said. "Now we go out for bigger game."

"Bigger is the operative word here," Grant said.

"How much bigger?" Janaina asked.

"Tree-smashing big. And it hunts to eat," Grant said.

"And that's why we have Mr. McCabe and his men with us," Katsoros said.

"Do you think that little wall of dirt around us will stop an animal that big?" Janaina said to Grant.

McCabe returned and cut in with an answer. "I just need to slow it down enough to get a clean shot. I've got rounds big enough to drop an elephant."

"This thing might be bigger than an elephant," Grant said.

Janaina turned to Katsoros. "And you think it's a good idea to go find this animal?"

"We don't need to find it, just traces of it," Katsoros said.

"That's right, we're here to scoop poop," Grant said.

"We'll give the animal a head start and Mr. McCabe will lead a group out in half an hour. Start at the attack site you found."

"It's more likely we'll find animal traces by water sources," Grant said.

"The trail went northwest," McCabe said, "toward the creek that runs out of the clearing."

"Then it's settled," Katsoros said.

"Your turn for some field work, Dixit?" Grant said.

"Hobart will be with you taking samples," Katsoros said. "Dr. Dixit will continue doing the analysis here with me."

"Yes, certainly," Dixit said. "The phoberomys analysis will be quite lengthy, indeed."

"Damn it, man," Grant said. "Hobart's injured. Maybe you let him tap on the keyboard while you scrape up dino dung."

"Dr. Coleman," Katsoros said. "Dr. Dixit is right to stay back. You're fit to go exploring, aren't you, Hobart?"

Hobart limped over, favoring his bandaged leg. "Yes, ma'am. Ready and able."

"Then we leave in thirty minutes," Katsoros said. "Everyone pack water and food for the day."

Grant shook his head in disgust and went to the supply pallet to refill his water bottle. Janaina followed.

"You are troubled?" she asked.

"That stupid kid is going to end up with some kind of infection in that animal bite after wandering around in the jungle. All because Katsoros wants to let Dixit play the chicken again. If he wants to work in a lab, he should have stayed back in a lab."

"It's Hobart's choice."

"But a good mentor would keep him from making a bad one."

"We'll have to keep an eye on the boy."

"We? You don't need to face that thing."

"I'm searching for other humans until I'm certain we are the only ones up here."

In a world filled with pterosaurs and whatever kind of behemoth eats giant guinea pigs, Grant doubted any primitive humans could survive here long.

Then he wondered how much better their odds would be.

***

The dinosaur's trail of crushed everything was easy for McCabe, Grant, Hobart, and Janaina to follow, and it did lead to the water. But what flowed like a creek in the clearing was more like a river when they got there. Other streams must have fed into it because it stretched a hundred meters wide and ran swift. No one would be doing any barefoot wading in it. The good news was that past surges in the water level had scoured the banks clear of vegetation, and they had a good line of sight on whatever they might be catching up with.

After a quick search, Grant had to swallow some pride and admit that he'd been wrong. They didn't see any signs of animals along the banks. No footprints, no nests. There might have been fish in the river, but after his experience with the fish in the Montana cavern, he was keeping his distance from the water.

"Hold up!" McCabe whispered.

He dropped to one knee on the sandy shore. The others followed. Grant's pulse quickened. McCabe brought a set of small binoculars to his eyes and trained them down river. Grant had no idea what the man was looking at. He couldn't see anything.

"Damn it," McCabe said. "Janaina, come here."

She scrambled over to him, and he handed her the binoculars. She trained them downstream. Her jaw dropped.

"*Ai, meu Deus*," she said. "There *are* people here."

Everyone crawled up beside Janaina. She passed the binoculars around. When it was Grant's turn he brought them up against his glasses with an embarrassing *thunk*. He kept them a few millimeters away and worked the focus. When it went razor sharp, he saw it too.

A suspension bridge across the stream.

A coating of leaves papered the bridge. There were no abutments on the stream, no supports in the center.

"How could anyone build that?" Hobart said.

"They started in the middle and worked out in both directions," Grant said.

"This is one of the beauties of these supposedly primitive societies," Janaina said. "Often they have amazing solutions to share. We're still not certain how the Easter Island monoliths came to be, or the great pyramids in Egypt."

McCabe took back the binoculars. He scanned both sides of the river. "Doesn't look like there's anyone here now. Good time to pass by."

"And solve the mystery of its construction," Janaina said.

McCabe led them downstream along the riverbank. The closer they got, the more bizarre the bridge became. There was no overhead suspension, no underlying trusses. Though the air was still, the bridge swayed ever so slightly, which only furthered the illusion that it was floating over the river. As they closed on it, the narrowness became apparent, and it ended up being under a meter wide. The group paused at the end. The leafy pavement made an almost imperceptible twist and return.

"Pretty damn narrow for people to walk across," Hobart said.

"And the lack of handrails would send an OSHA inspector screaming," Grant said.

"Doesn't look like anyone's been walking across," McCabe said. "No footprints in the sand."

Indeed, there weren't any, on either side. Instead, tiny holes speckled the sand, like someone had pricked it all over with a stick.

Hobart dropped his backpack and knelt down to inspect the top of the bridge. He grabbed one leaf. It appeared to be coated with half-dried glue. The bridge shuddered. He peeled the leaf up.

The head of an enormous ant popped up and hissed at him.

He jerked back and ripped the leaf clean away. Several other leaves came with it. The opening exposed the inner structure of the bridge. All ants, rosy red and a meter long, with leaves glued to their backs. A hissing chorus spit from the leafy tube of the bridge.

A deeper hiss responded from back in the jungle.

"Pull back," McCabe said. "Right now!"

The four dashed back up the riverbank and into the underbrush. They dropped flat on the spongy ground. Grant held his breath.

The sound of breaking leaves and snapping twigs came closer. Hobart's head began to tremble. He raised himself up to make a run for it. McCabe grabbed him by the shirt and yanked him back down with a thud.

"Too late for that now," McCabe whispered.

Two sharp little squeals punctuated the sounds of something big breaking trail. Grant buried his face in the dirt, wishing he could burrow completely into it.

The train of something marched past them, so close that bushes right in front of the group rustled. But the intruders passed by and headed for the river.

When the noise stopped, Grant crawled over for a better view of the bridge. Four ants, twice as large as the ones they'd uncovered, trooped toward the bridge. They were a darker, ruby red, with mandibles as long as a man's forearm. Clamped in each set wriggled a phoberomys. The ants marched single file across the leaf-bridge and into the jungle on the far bank.

Leaves rustled behind Grant, then came another hiss, deeper, more like a roar. The heads of three more ants thrust out of the bushes. Their mandibles stretched wide open and the razor-sharp edges sparkled in the sunlight.

Grant and the others broke and ran down the riverbank. The ants charged after them.

Janaina and Grant dashed for the water. Hobart cut the other way. His weight shifted hard to his injured leg. He screamed, stopped, and dropped to one knee.

McCabe spun to face the ants at the water's edge. He snapped his rifle to his shoulder and fired at the lead ant. The creature's head exploded like a ripe melon. The rear segments kept charging forward.

McCabe stepped aside, aimed at the ant to his left and fired again. This round disintegrated the middle segment. The other two fell on their sides, legs flailing in the air. The mandibles on the head snapped furiously at nothing.

The third ant moved too fast. By the time McCabe turned to it, it had clamped on Hobart's leg. The mandibles sliced through his thigh like shears snipping a rose stem. Hobart shrieked. Blood spurted and splattered the ant's head and antennae. The ant jerked its head and tore Hobart's leg free. The technician collapsed.

The ant reared its head high, leg clamped in its mandibles. McCabe fired twice. Bullets tore through the ant's head and thorax. It spun to the ground, dead.

From across the river came a chorus of hisses. A half-dozen more soldier ants scurried out of the jungle and charged single file across the bridge.

McCabe swiveled to the bridge, aimed, and fired. The shot missed and blasted through the leaves coating the bridge's center. The structure shuddered and the soldier ants paused to get stable.

Grant had an idea. He drew his machete and dashed to the end of the bridge. Several ants clamped the riverbank from under the leaves' edges. With one swipe he slashed at the insects. Ant legs snapped like match sticks. A hissing head popped up near Grant's foot. He chopped again at the bridge. More legs splintered and then the bridge collapsed. The soldier ants skidded sideways off the canted leaves and splashed into the river. The bridge dissolved into a swarm of leaf-covered ants thrashing in the water as the current pulled them downstream.

Grant sighed with relief. Janaina ran to Hobart. Twenty meters downstream, a bridge ant, water-soaked leaf draped over its back, crawled up on Grant's side of the river. McCabe dispatched it with one shot.

Grant went to help Janaina with Hobart, but his gray skin and clouded eyes said that they were both too late. He was dead.

"What the hell was all that?" McCabe said. "Since when do ants act like steel girders?"

"Army ants do," Janaina said. "They build living bridges like that to cross obstacles. And the leaves? Weaver ants excrete silk and build whole nests that way. These ants have adapted to use the leaves for traction, or perhaps protection from the sun while hanging in place. The stronger soldier ants were likely bringing back food for the colony."

"Is bringing live food another normal ant thing to do?" Grant said.

"No, that's very different."

"Nice to see them wash downstream," McCabe said.

"I'm certain they will be back," Janaina said. "Ants communicate with each other using pheromones and body movements. The survivors will return to the colony and tell what happened here. Scouts will return to the water obstacle, and then the colony will start the rebuilding."

"Let's not be here when they do," McCabe said.

Janaina looked up, eye welling with tears. "What about Hobart? We can't just leave him here."

"I'm not carrying a corpse through the jungle," McCabe said.

"You would if it was one of your men."

"You bet your ass I would. But he isn't."

Janaina looked to Grant for support.

Grant sighed. "I hate it but McCabe's right. We have no way to carry him."

Janaina shot Grant a cold stare.

"We'll come back for the body," Grant said.

"Or whatever's left after the ants pick him clean," McCabe said. "We need to pull back and carry more firepower if we're going dinosaur hunting."

Hobart's backpack lay on the sandy riverbank. Grant picked it up and walked back to Hobart's body.

"What are you doing?" McCabe said.

"Making sure that the guy didn't die for nothing. I'm bringing back a sample."

Grant stepped over to the corpse of the ant that killed Hobart. Hobart's severed leg lay beside the creature's head. Grant raised his machete and with two blows severed the long mandibles from the creature's head. A third well-aimed chop severed the head from the rest of the body. He opened the pack and scooped the head up inside it. The big head was a tight fit. Grant shouldered the pack and it felt like he was carrying an oversized bowling ball. He cinched the straps tight.

He wished they were leaving cowardly Dixit's body on the ground instead of Hobart's. He didn't feel guilty about wishing it.

CHAPTER FOURTEEN

When they returned to camp, the berm around the site had an extra layer of tree trunks and branches around the crest. The Bobcat was recharging by the solar panels. Griggs had fashioned a crude ladder and now stood guard atop the shipping container. He gave the group an all-clear thumbs-up and waved them in through a narrow gap in the trunks. The three scaled the berm and slid down the other side.

Katsoros met them at the container. Her eyes narrowed. "Where's Hobart?"

"Killed by giant ants," Grant said. He threw the backpack at her feet. "But we got a sample of one, so it's all worth it, right?"

Katsoros gave the backpack a grim look. "Where's Hobart's body?"

"In the jungle. We'll need to fashion some kind of a stretcher and go back and get it."

"No we won't."

"What?"

"We can't risk lives over a life already lost. Any more casualties and we might not complete the task at hand."

"He wouldn't be a casualty if you'd sent Dixit. Hobart's leg injury cost him his life."

Katsoros looked at McCabe. He shrugged. "Might have got him anyway. Ants moved fast."

Katsoros put a hand on Grant's shoulder. "I'm sorry that Hobart was killed. Believe me. At least you thought to get this sample of the ant."

Grant shook off Katsoros's hand. "I'm going to make sure Dixit knows what this sample cost."

He grabbed the backpack from the ground and stormed over to where Dixit sat engrossed in a laptop screen. Grant unzipped the pack and dumped the ant head in Dixit's lap. Dixit yelped, jumped to his feet, and scrambled backwards. The head rolled to a stop, face up, black, glassy eyes staring at Dixit.

"That thing killed Hobart," Grant said.

"H-how?"

"Giant ants attacked us at the river. McCabe shot two but the third one bit Hobart before McCabe killed it. You're the one who should have been out there. His death is on you."

Dixit took a breath and exhaled. "I cannot control what wild beasts do. Or people's reaction to them. This is a most dangerous location."

"You bastard. Now next time you need a sample of something, you'll be getting it yourself. We'll see how the 'wild beasts' treat you."

Grant scooped the pack off the ground and left Dixit staring at the severed ant head. He stomped off to a spot in the shadow of the sleeping container, tossed the pack aside, and slumped to the ground. A thick yellow card with a clip on one end fluttered out. Grant picked it up.

The card had a Transworld logo on one side. On the other were five squares. Each square had a number in it. 5, 10, 25, 50, 100. The square with the 5 was filled in green, the rest were clear.

More Transworld nonsense. He threw the card back in the backpack. Nothing about the expedition was working out as expected. And he was starting to wonder if there was more to the objective than he'd been told.

CHAPTER FIFTEEN

Later that afternoon, Grant carried a small canvas roll in his hands as he approached the container. Inside were his tools for unearthing and preparing fossils. They weren't even close to correct for what he was about to do, but this place was the land of making do. Janaina sat slumped against the container on the sliver of shade the afternoon sun provided. He walked over.

"I've seen engineering students in English Lit classes look more enthusiastic than you do right now," he said.

She managed a small smile. "Well, I just watched someone get shredded by ants. And I'm here to manage the contact with any indigenous peoples, but unless they come climbing up the cliff face, I don't really have anything to do except wait to be killed by some formerly extinct species."

"You said you earned a degree before you turned to working for the indigenous peoples, right?"

"Two biology degrees, actually."

"Let's put them to work." He tossed her the pack of tools. "Want to help me examine that pterosaur?"

Her face brightened. "Absolutely! Will Dr. Dixit allow it?"

"If he hasn't harvested what little he needs for testing by now, he can get back in line behind us."

Janaina jumped up and followed Grant back to the work area. Dixit was pounding away at keys on his laptop when they arrived. Grant went to the electric cooler where Dixit kept his samples.

"We're going to do a post-mortem on the pterosaur," Grant said. "Okay with you?"

Dixit bolted upright. "Certainly not. I may need more samples in the future and your chopping at it would contaminate—"

"Excellent! Thanks!" Grant popped open the cooler and pulled the pterosaur's sample bag out. He dumped the corpse on the top of the cooler and rubbed his hands across the back. "Oops. Contamination. We'll take this off your hands."

Grant scooped up the pterosaur and took it over to the top of a shipping crate. Janaina followed with Grant's tools. In the jungle heat, the dinosaur rapidly thawed. And just as rapidly began to stink.

"Wow," Janaina said. "I thought they smelled bad when they were alive."

"Could you get me a couple of rocks the size of your fist?"

Janaina stepped away and Grant unfolded the wings. They stretched out over a meter. Janaina returned with the rocks and Grant used them like paperweights to pin the wings in place.

"Except for the thicker haunch and leg muscles," Grant said, "this is very close to what we thought pterosaurs looked like based on the fossil record. And it settles the question of whether they had feathers or not."

"Unless it is molting season," Janaina said.

Grant raised an eyebrow as he considered the idea. Janaina broke out laughing and punched him in the shoulder.

"I am, how you say, messing with you," she said. "That is how you paleontologists work, always creating one nonsense conjecture after another. We biologists prefer observations and common sense. Of course this creature never has feathers."

"Maybe you should go back to sitting in the shade."

Janaina took one of the knives and sliced open a leg. "These are running muscles, like a dog, not launching muscles like a hawk. And we certainly saw them run."

"As soon as I get back, I want to look much more closely at the fossil record, see if that's evolution at work here or if the fossils have the same attachment pattern for tendons."

Grant examined the bill. The bottom half had a hole in the center that ran upward into the bill. He pried open the mouth, but it did not appear connected. "That hole is nothing I've ever seen in any fossils."

"It doesn't appear to help eating or respiration," Janaina said.

"And there's another mystery I'd like to solve. This long extension behind the head. It seems to balance the bill, but modern birds like toucans have long bills and need no counterweight."

Janaina ran the knife along the length of the head crest. She pulled back the leathery skin to expose white bone.

"The two theories are that it either helped stabilize them in flight," Grant said, "or the hollow space is an extension of the olfactory area, an enormous space to trap scent and locate prey."

"I need a bone saw."

"I have a chisel. You might want to step back."

Grant picked up a small chisel and a hammer. He set the chisel's tip perpendicular to the base of the head crest and gave it a sharp smack with the hammer. The head crest split all the way to the top. Using the chisel and a pick, Grant pried open the bone.

The space inside the bone was not hollow. A gray mass filled the area. The surface had tiny creases all along it, except at the very tip, where there were well defined folds.

"Damn," Grant said. "That looks like a brain."

"But not a bird's brain," Janaina said. "A bird's brain surface is smooth. These creases and folds indicate much higher brain function. This is more like the brain of a mammal."

"Like a human?"

"No, ours are much more complex." She pointed the knife at the more creased tip. "Except for that section. That puts our brain to shame."

"What would that part do?"

"No idea. But whatever it does, a pterosaur does it better than we do it."

Katsoros approached the shipping container. "What stinks so badly?" She took a look at the partially dissected pterosaur. "Ugh. What are you two doing?"

"We call it science," Grant said. "It's what you signed me up to do."

McCabe marched over before Katsoros could reply. The wretched stink of the pterosaur didn't seem to faze him.

"We still have a problem," he said. "No communication with our pickup plane."

"Once they see the airstrip…" Katsoros said.

"*If* they see the airstrip. And I know Kowolski, who owns the air charter. He takes few chances to begin with, and even doing that, he's down one plane. Without proof of life, he's going to turn around and head home getting the exact same paycheck."

"The pterosaurs have the radio," Grant said. "I'm sure if we ask for it nicely…"

"Are there other radios in the plane?" Katsoros asked.

"None that will use the right frequencies. But Riffaud had an idea. He noticed that the plane had chaff dispensers."

"What's chaff?"

"It's made up of strips like aluminum foil. It gets loaded in tubes along the tail of the plane. When you blast it out of the tube, it makes a cloud that gets picked up by radar. It confuses anti-aircraft systems."

"Why would that plane have to confuse anti-aircraft systems?" Grant said.

"What Kowalski did on his trips into Columbia was his own business," McCabe said. "My point is that we can use those tubes to signal the plane. Mount them in the ground, fire them straight up. In this big open sky, an incoming pilot might miss a tiny red flare. There's no way he'd miss his terrain radar suddenly saying there's a mountain in front of him."

"How large might these things be?" Dixit said.

"Small enough, even you can carry one or two," McCabe said.

"Wow, miniature, huh?" Grant said.

"There's no way we'll get back to that plane," Katsoros said. "Pterosaurs will be all over us."

"Dino Doc says they are not nocturnal. We go at night."

"Whoa," Grant said. "I *hypothesized* they were diurnal. No guarantee they aren't active some of the night, like we are."

"Anyone has a better plan, I'm open to it. But if we don't have a way to signal that plane, we're going to have to find a way to live off pterosaur wings and phoberomys stew for the rest of our lives."

No one said a thing.

With no better options, Grant resigned himself to the plan. "What time do we leave?"

"You aren't going anywhere. The last thing I need is some scary story writer crashing through the jungle like you did all day yesterday. Riffaud and I have been moving silently in the dark for decades. We'll leave two hours after sunset. We'll slip in and out before anything knows we've left the compound."

Grant wanted to raise a protest at this assault on his manly skills in front of Katsoros and Janaina. But on the other hand, a night trip through a dinosaur infested jungle wasn't that great an idea to start with.

"Whatever you say," Grant said.

CHAPTER SIXTEEN

After an hour of trying that night, Grant gave up on going to sleep. Janaina, Dixit, and Katsoros were able to strap in and drift off, but Grant's mind was running full speed with concerns about McCabe and Riffaud surviving the jungle, the odds of the group being rescued, Hobart's death, and the inhumanity of leaving his body as ant food at the river. He raised himself from the seat without a sound and crept out of the container.

The half-moon in the clear sky cast enough light to make out the bigger shapes in the compound. He checked the top of the container for Griggs, but it was empty. He guessed that Griggs was probably walking the perimeter. He headed out to the berm and climbed to the top.

He peered out between two tree limbs. Across the clearing around the berm, the moonlight did nothing against the impenetrable darkness of the jungle. He had no idea how McCabe and Riffaud would get to the airplane wreck and back. But they treated the mission like just another day, so it must have been one of their military skills he didn't fathom.

He'd spent plenty of nights outdoors, months at a time at fossil excavations, in places darker than this. But no place had ever felt this unnerving. A combination of the unknown species out there and the complete isolation from the rest of the world gave him a helpless feeling he hadn't had since the experiences that spawned *Cavern of the Damned*. Knowing how that worked out didn't make him feel any better.

"What are you doing out here?"

Griggs's voice startled him and he slammed his head against a tree limb.

"Ow, damn. I thought you might need company."

"Uh, no. I'm fine alone."

"Then I guess I thought I needed company."

"There's three other people back in the container."

"They're asleep."

"Follow their lead."

Something crashed in the jungle out in front of them.

Griggs snapped his rifle's safety off and aimed the barrel over the top tree limb. Grant looked across the clearing and saw nothing but black standing in for the jungle he knew was out there.

More leaves rustled and a branch snapped.

"How big does whatever's out there sound to you, Doc?"

"Too big."

Griggs pulled his revolver from its holster and handed it to Grant grip-first. "Take this and stay low."

Grant hesitated, then took it. It weighed a lot more than he'd expected. "I haven't shot one of these before."

"Point and pull the trigger," Griggs said. "I have a feeling whatever's coming will be big enough that you won't miss."

A tree at the jungle's edge toppled over and slammed into the ground. From behind it charged a saucer-shaped hulk the size of a car. The shape resembled a turtle, but it didn't move like one. Stubby legs threw sprays of earth past its sides. It ran straight for the berm.

Griggs snapped on a rifle-mounted flashlight. The beam lit up an ankylosaur. Armored plates covered its broad back and the crest of its head. Defensive spikes jutted from the edges of both. A ball at the end of its long tail bounced off the ground as it charged.

Griggs opened fire. A spray of bullets barked from his rifle. The rounds hit the creature square in the back to no effect. One of the spent shell casings winged Grant in the head.

The hulk beneath them turned sideways and slipped mostly under Grant's line of sight. Then the creature slammed the club on its tail into the earth. The berm shuddered and Grant grabbed a tree limb to hold his balance. Griggs pointed his rifle straight over the edge and fired without aiming.

The ankylosaur's head shot up above the berm and into the beam of Griggs's light. Its huge beak spread wide and revealed a thick, forked tongue. A yellow eye with a snake's slit iris stared both men down. The creature uttered a guttural roar and its hot breath stank of things long dead. It swung its head and its beak hit Griggs. The rifle flew from the man's hands. The flashlight's beam cartwheeled through the air as the weapon tumbled down the berm.

Grant realized he still held the revolver in his sweaty, trembling hand. He raised it and pulled the trigger. Just a meter from the creature he couldn't miss. The bullet hit the back armor and pinged as it deflected away. The kick from the revolver nearly knocked Grant off the berm.

Griggs whipped a hunting knife from a sheath at his belt. With an overhand sweep, he plunged it into the ankylosaur's eye.

The creature screeched like shearing metal. It swept its head in Griggs direction, but he ducked just in time. The creature dropped down from the berm. It bellowed in fury and the sound of churning earth rolled up from the darkness as the dinosaur no doubt tried to dislodge the knife in its eye. A crunch of metal sounded to the west and then the ankylosaur barreled off into the jungle.

Grant's pulse hammered so hard he could feel his body jerk in time with it. The revolver shook in his hand. The silence in the wake of the creature's departure now seemed unnatural.

"Dammit," Griggs said. "That was my favorite knife." He turned to Grant. "You okay?"

"Yeah… yeah. That was close."

Griggs eased the pistol out of Grant's hand. "Let me hold this for now."

Grant wasn't in the mood to argue. He let the pistol go.

"What happened up there?" Katsoros called from the base on the berm. She scooped up Griggs' rifle.

"Animal attack." Griggs called down. "Repelled it." He looked to Grant. "Good job."

"I shot it once."

"But you didn't run."

Grant got the feeling this was as close to praise as a civilian was likely to get from Griggs, so he opted to take it without a smart-ass or self-deprecating response.

They slid down the berm. By the time they got there Janaina and Dixit had joined Katsoros.

"What was it?" Katsoros said.

"Ankylosaurus," Grant said. "Basically an armored car with a dinosaur inside."

"Did you kill it?" Dixit asked.

"No, but we sure did irritate it."

"It's wounded," Griggs said. "Blind in one eye."

"You think this was what was hunting the phoberomys the night before last?"

"From the looks of it, yes. Which means it isn't the normal, placid, plant-eating version. And the crushed eggs might be ankylosaurs as well. We've disturbed its hunting and killed its family. No wonder it has a bad attitude."

"Can you kill it if it comes back?" Janaina asked Griggs.

"Not by myself," Griggs said.

Grant bristled at being demoted back to useless.

"It would take all three of us, thick as that armor is. When McCabe and Riffaud return, we'll have a chance."

Grant wondered if McCabe and Riffaud would return. Were there other ankylosaurs out there on the rampage tonight?

CHAPTER SEVENTEEN

Two hours later, Janaina, Katsoros, and Dixit had gone back to sleep. If Grant couldn't sleep before the dinosaur attack, he sure wasn't doing it after. He and Griggs sat on top of the container. Griggs had his rifle across his lap, his legs dangled over the side. Grant could barely see anything in the moonlight. He hoped Griggs had some sort of bionic night-vision the military had installed because if it was up to Grant to spot the next attack, it wouldn't happen until the thing was knocking over the container.

While Grant kept a swiveling scan of the perimeter going, Griggs stayed focused on one location.

"You expecting the dinosaur to hit us from that direction?" Grant asked.

"No, I'm expecting McCabe and Riffaud from that direction. The opening between the tree trunks on top of the berm is the only passage point in and out of camp. Anything that pops up somewhere else on the other side gets shot."

"Good idea. Hey, why didn't I know about that?"

"A lot of security measures go on behind the client's back. It's better that way. They don't interfere."

"Yeah, but what if I was outside and decided to come back in a different way?"

"That's why you aren't allowed outside the perimeter without adult supervision."

McCabe's voice drifted in from the other side of the berm. "Griggs! Coming in!"

"Clear!" Griggs shouted back.

Seconds later McCabe appeared atop the berm, followed by Riffaud. Each had a metal tube about a meter and a half long strapped across their backs. They skidded down the berm. Griggs hopped off the container to meet them. Grant measured the drop in his head and took the more judicious route of the makeshift ladder. He caught up as Griggs and McCabe fist bumped.

"Give me a sit rep," McCabe snapped. "What the hell happened out there? The ground all around the berm looks like a minefield exploded."

"Dinosaur outside the perimeter," Griggs said. "Armored up like an APC."

"Did you light it up?"

"Thirty rounds, center of mass, couldn't miss the thing. It didn't flinch."

"What was it, Dino Doc?"

"An ankylosaur," Grant said, "or some evolutionary one-off."

"Wide and low to the ground," Griggs said. "Gonna be tough to kill."

"You think it was the thing that slaughtered the guinea pigs?" McCabe said.

Grant cringed at calling the animals guinea pigs, but held back his correction. "That would be a safe bet."

McCabe checked the glowing face of his watch. "We have dawn in a few hours. Griggs, get some sleep. We need the landing strip done ASAP." He slung the launcher off his back and handed it to Riffaud. "You drop the launchers by the supply pallet and watch the perimeter. I'll wire them up in the morning."

Grant waited for an assignment.

"Okay, move out," McCabe said. The three men split to complete their tasks and left Grant standing alone.

"I'll head back in and get a little sleep," Grant said to no one.

CHAPTER EIGHTEEN

Dawn brought Grant back around, and earlier than he'd hoped. He unstrapped himself from the sleep chair and went outside. Riffaud stood guard atop the container. Grant gave him a friendly wave. Riffaud gave an exasperated sigh in response.

"Okay, next time *you* fend off the dinosaur attack," Grant whispered to himself. He climbed up to the top of the berm to get a better view of last night's battlefield.

It looked as bad as he'd guessed. Ground all churned up. Trees across the way flattened. He peered down the far side of the berm and couldn't miss the cavity the clubbed tail of the ankylosaur had crushed into it. They'd need the Bobcat to get it back in shape.

He looked over to where the Bobcat always spent the night charging. The little excavator was ten meters further out in the field, on its side. The side facing up had the same size dent in it that the ankylosaur had put in the berm. The ground for a hundred meters around the Bobcat was nothing but clumps of earth and uprooted plants.

Griggs stood up from behind it. He slammed a fist against the cage and then gave the front a kick for good measure. Grant couldn't hear what he was saying, but he could make an educated guess that it was profane. The Bobcat looked down for the count.

Katsoros was the next one awake. As soon as she was out the door, she pulled her arm from her bandana sling and tried to stretch it. Her face screwed up in pain and she put it back in the sling. Then McCabe joined her from who knew where. Grant seriously considered whether the guy could make himself invisible at will. He climbed down off the berm.

"The Bobcat's tango uniform," McCabe said.

"Which means?"

"Dino Doc's visitor last night destroyed it."

Dixit and Janaina, rubbing sleep from their eyes, joined the group.

"My visitor?" Grant said. "Griggs was the one who ran over its nest and made us the bad guys."

"Is the airstrip long enough yet?" Katsoros said.

"Barely. If they have a good pilot. And they get some sort of signal that we're alive down here to make it worth the risk to try."

"Then you need to get those chaff tubes ready to fire," Katsoros said. "And I need to go home mission complete. We need an ankylosaur sample to cross reference with the others."

"I doubt it will give that up voluntarily," Grant said.

"There are probably blood and skin samples on the Bobcat." She looked at Grant.

"No way in hell," Grant said. "For once Dixit can do his own work. The Bobcat isn't even a hundred yards away."

"That will be agreeable," Dixit said. "I shall gather the samples myself."

"And I'll go with you," Katsoros said.

The two walked away together, and Grant felt like a jerk for refusing to do such a simple task. McCabe climbed up to the top of the berm and shouted for Griggs to come back in.

Janaina stepped up beside Grant. She didn't say a word, but he could practically smell the disgust and disappointment the boiled inside her about how he'd just treated Dixit.

"I'm sorry about my response there. I was a little rough on Dixit."

"No, you were childish."

"I'll go get the samples."

"Not now you are not. You forced him into it and he'll have to do it to prove you wrong."

"So I have to let him go and still be responsible if he dies."

"How you say, 'on the nose'."

"Now I feel much better about the situation." Grant shifted the conversation topic. "I've been thinking about those totems we found when we first arrived. I wonder if they are an apatosaurus, or the raised tail of an ankylosaurus."

Janaina thought it over. "Yes, that could be correct."

"If there were apatosaurs here, we'd have seen signs of them, and this plateau doesn't have the large, shallow water system a big sauropod would need."

"It is also more likely that the people would fear the aggressive ankylosaur, and do magic to keep it up here away from them. Perhaps one fell off the cliff somewhere back in time. The people came across this dead monster from the sky, and decided they didn't want to have any more of that happening."

"With Dixit out gathering samples, let's put that workspace to use and do some science."

"Such as?"

"There's the ant head we brought back from the bridge incident. My tools are back there. Let's dissect it."

Janaina smiled. "Yes. A good use of our time."

They went to the work area. Grant opened up the storage chest.

The head sat inside, staring up at nothing with its solid black eyes. The glossy exoskeleton looked almost artificial. He unrolled his pack of tools.

Janaina grabbed his arm. "Oh my God. That head just moved."

"The head can't move. The thing has been dead for a day."

Grant picked the head up from the cooler. The exoskeleton felt cold and smooth as fine china. "See, dead is—"

The head shook in his hands.

"Holy hell!"

He threw the head down like it had been electrically charged. It hit the ground with a sharp crack and an inch-wide split opened up that ran right between the ant's eyes. It didn't move again.

"I think I killed it," he said.

"You were just telling me it was already dead."

Grant pulled two picks from his tool kit. He'd done enough touching of this thing already. He wedged the tips into the crack in the head and spread it wide. The head opened with a snap. A rank smell like rotten meat exhaled into Grant's face.

"*Ai, meu Deus.*" Janaina turned away and covered her mouth.

Grant held his breath and pulled again. The head split fully open. Whatever had passed for a brain in the creature had decayed to a gray mass of goo. But in the center of that mass wiggled an eight-centimeter long, white larvae. It raised its head and stared at Grant with two unblinking black eye spots.

His first instinct was to crush it. The slimy skin, the faceless head, the fact that it writhed in a puddle of decaying brain matter—all this inspired some primal self-defense mechanism. But as the impulse became overwhelming, the creature's skin browned. It shuddered, then collapsed into the mess it had been feeding upon. Green fluid seeped out of its mouth, and it lay still.

"Ugh, is that some Amazonian maggot?" Grant asked.

"If it is, it's not from any species I know of," Janaina said. "I'd hate to see what it pupates into."

"Just when I was hoping the saving grace of this place was a low number of insect species. Let's see what Dixit can make of it."

Grant took a sample bag from a supply box and opened it. Using the two picks, he pinched the larva in the middle, raised it, and plopped it into the bag. He zipped the bag shut. His first impulse was to drop it on Dixit's closed laptop. Already feeling guilty about having shamed Dixit into leaving the safety of the compound, he set the larva beside the computer instead.

"That was good of you," Janaina said.

"What?"

"I have two younger brothers. I know the look of someone thinking of doing something bad and then having their conscience pull them back. You were going to leave that on his laptop."

"Me? Never."

She shook her head. "Stick with that story if you wish."

"Now I'm committed to it."

CHAPTER NINETEEN

Grant felt worse than ever about Dixit being outside the perimeter now that Janaina had called him on his temptation to do something childish with the larva. He headed over to the berm to see how the poor guy was progressing. McCabe already stood atop the earthen barricade, facing the wrecked Bobcat. Grant climbed up next to him.

"Talk about sitting ducks," McCabe said. "A woman with her arm in a sling and a guy who can barely walk across that field without tripping over his own feet. They should have asked you to do that sampling. You'd have been done already."

Grant was afraid to say anything to that. Instead he watched Katsoros pace back and forth by the front of the Bobcat. Dixit swabbed some blood and cells from the frame of the Bobcat and stuck the swab in a plastic bag. He very precisely zipped closed the bag. Then he laid it on the Bobcat, took a sharpie from his pocket and removed the cap. Then he started to label the sample bag.

"For Pete's sake, man," Grant whispered. "You know where the damn sample came from. Stop wasting time."

Katsoros gave Dixit a similar, more fiery reaction, blessedly muffled by the distance from the berm to the Bobcat. Dixit put the sample in his pocket.

The earth around Katsoros shuddered, then the ripple spread out past the Bobcat into the shape of a giant plate.

"Run!" Grant shouted.

The head of the ankylosaurus burst from the ground at Katsoros's feet and she slammed back into the Bobcat. Griggs's knife still stuck from the creature's left eye. Its beak opened and it let loose a furious roar. Dixit broke into a panicked, spastic scramble where much effort seemed to provide little forward motion.

The ankylosaur rose from the beneath the earth, and with a great shake sent dirt and uprooted plants swirling off its armored back. Katsoros ran for the compound. The dinosaur cocked its good eye at the two retreating humans and roared again.

McCabe aimed at the dinosaur's head. It dipped its beak and the rounds slammed into its armored cover to no effect. The beast charged.

Dixit made it to the berm first. Half way up, the soft earth gave way. Grant reached over a tree trunk and stretched out a hand to him. Dixit grabbed it, and Grant pulled.

Katsoros was halfway to the berm, but the dinosaur was faster. It caught up to her, and with a swipe of its head sent her flying sideways. She spun across the earth, arms and legs out like a human pinwheel, then stopped dead still. The dinosaur twisted its head left to see where its prey had landed.

Its stretch exposed a wide swath of unarmored skin along its neck. McCabe aimed fast and sent a blizzard of rounds at this natural weak spot. Bullets peppered the creature's neck and sent geysers of blood into the air. The dinosaur swung back to face the compound with a furious scream. Cold as ice, McCabe shifted his aim and sent three rounds into its right eye.

The ankylosaur rose up on its hind feet and spun to make a retreat. It sent the club of its tail sailing toward the top of the berm.

Grant pulled a struggling Dixit up and over the log at the berm's crown. Dixit tumbled down the other side. Grant dropped flat and buried his face in the dirt. McCabe dove forward and tucked into a combat roll down the outside.

The beast's club tail raked through the obstacles at the top of the berm. Tree trunks snapped like matchsticks. The club passed so close to Grant's head that the breeze ruffled his hair. In a tornado of shattered branches and limbs, the dinosaur swept clean the section of the berm where the men had been standing.

Grant looked down to see the ankylosaur run for the cover of the jungle, bowling over trees and bushes as it left the clearing. McCabe kept it in his sights until it disappeared. Then he ran for Katsoros. He slung his weapon across his back, scooped her up in a fireman's carry and charged back up the berm. He didn't set her down until he was on the other side. Grant skidded down the berm after him.

Rich, red blood coated the left side of Katsoros' head. Her neck bent at an impossible angle and she didn't move. McCabe checked her for a pulse but it was obvious that the effort wasn't necessary.

"Dammit," McCabe whispered.

Dixit staggered over. Janaina arrived at a run. Griggs displayed the soldier's reaction and ran straight by them to take a defensive position on the berm.

"What happened?" Janaina said.

"The ankylosaur," Grant said. "It buried itself in the dirt like a rockfish in sand. It used the bashed Bobcat as bait and ambushed Dixit and Katsoros."

"Did you kill it?" Janaina asked McCabe.

"No, but I wounded it pretty bad. It knows what's in store for it if it comes back."

McCabe said that like the injury would be a deterrent. Grant thought the wounds were just one more reason for it to want revenge.

Something rectangular stuck out of Katsoros' pocket, attached to her belt loop with a lanyard. Grant pulled it out. It was the same kind of card he'd found in Hobart's pack. But on this one, both the five and the ten boxes had turned green. He looked up at the still shuddering Dixit.

"What are these things?"

"I've seen those," McCabe answered. "Used them in ops in Iraq. They're personal dosimeters. Radiation detectors."

"Radiation?" Janaina said.

Grant cast an accusatory look at Dixit. He noticed a lanyard looped around Dixit's belt and going into his pocket. Grant yanked on it and a dosimeter popped out of his pocket. McCabe sprang to his feet, unholstered his pistol and pointed it at Dixit.

"What the hell did you get us into here?" McCabe said.

Dixit raised his hands. "Transworld found uranium here. Possibly a lot of it. Enough to make it worth extracting." He reached down and tapped the dosimeter. "These are just to monitor the ground levels. A precautionary measure. You can see the levels are quite satisfactory."

"Anything above zero is quite unsatisfactory," Grant said. He turned to McCabe. "Are you in on this scheme?"

"It's news to me," McCabe said with a level of controlled fury that convinced Grant that he was telling the truth.

Grant put it together in his head. "These were in the messenger bag she retrieved from the plane wreck. That was what was so important that she'd risk her life and couldn't trust one of us to bring it back without opening it."

Dixit nodded.

"So all this talk about discovering extinct species and using their DNA for the good of mankind is all crap," Janaina said. "Transworld is here for uranium." She turned to Dixit. "Then what is it you're doing?"

Grant stood up so he could look down on the man and add a little intimidation.

"I am doing just what I have said," Dixit said. "Cataloging DNA. You have seen me working."

"Working on what?"

Dixit hesitated. "A poison. One that targets their DNA, and is benign to ours."

"We discover all these amazing creatures and your plan is to slaughter them?"

"The benefits of this place are under the ground, not above it. Isn't the proof in that everything here has tried to kill us? Reveal these creatures to the world and Transworld loses everything invested here."

"Were you going to kill all of us to keep this secret?" Janaina said.

"No one would talk. You signed non-disclosure agreements. Plus Transworld would pay you all to keep the secret. The mercenaries would accept. Janaina, your payment would go to save indigenous tribes, so you'd accept."

"I wouldn't," Grant said.

"You are the writer of monster stories. Who would believe you?"

"You're crazy if you think I'm letting you finish your research," Grant said.

"You'd better hope he does," McCabe said. "Our ammo isn't unlimited and we're outnumbered hundreds to one. That guy's poison might be the only way we survive."

"If radiation exposure doesn't kill us," Grant said.

"The badges say we are quite within prescribed parameters," Dixit said.

"And I'm not planning on any long-term exposure," McCabe said.

"I wonder if low level radiation contributed to the kinds of creatures we've encountered?" Janaina said.

"It wouldn't make the ants giants," Grant said. "It's not like some 1950s movie. But it would spur mutations that would accelerate evolution, explaining the changes in species here from what we've seen in fossil records."

"Then why *are* the ants giants?"

"There has to be some evolutionary benefit that enlarged them over millions of years. A lack of predators? A type of food source? Who knows."

"Can we prioritize staying alive over your egghead research?" McCabe said. "Dixit, have you got what you need to kill these damn things or not?"

"I have a multitude of concentrated compounds in two cases by the sample cooler. The research will yield the proper combination."

"Well stop wasting time jaw-jacking," McCabe said. "We're going to need that poison."

CHAPTER TWENTY

With the Bobcat trashed and the team down two people, the main mission had been reduced to survival. Grant showed Dixit the larva and explained that he and Janaina had extracted it from the head of a soldier ant. The soldiers walked the perimeter berm. Janaina gave Dixit what help she could.

Dixit didn't want Grant near him, and Grant understood completely. He wasn't thrilled about being near himself right now. He'd done exactly what Janaina had warned him not to do—let his emotional reaction to Dixit get in the way of the job they had to do. He hated himself for it and the results of it. So while the others added value, he sat in the shade of the container and felt useless.

McCabe approached from the berm. Grant figured that the only reason McCabe would be coming over was to give him a healthy ration of crap about something, likely about sending Katsoros out to her death with Dixit. Grant wished for someplace to hide. He stared at the ground. McCabe stopped, towering over Grant.

"This place is more dangerous than you thought, isn't it," McCabe said.

"More than any of us thought."

McCabe drew his pistol from its holster. Grant looked up and waited for the cold barrel to jab him in the forehead.

Instead, McCabe flipped it around and pointed the butt at Grant.

"Understand you acquitted yourself damn well with one of these on the berm," McCabe said. "We'll need all hands armed and ready when that thing comes back."

"Uh, thanks." Grant took the pistol.

McCabe unclipped the holster from his belt. "And you'd better take this. I expect to get that back in one piece when we get the hell out of here."

Grant stood and accepted the holster. "Yes, sir."

"But so help me God, you accidentally shoot me or someone else with this weapon, you'll be the next one it kills. Are we clear?"

"Clear as a summer day."

McCabe nodded and returned to the berm. Grant tucked the pistol into the holster and hung it on his belt. The weight made him feel a bit lopsided. He rested a hand on the pistol. The last time he'd had a gun at his side like this, it was hard plastic and he was a seven-year-old in a Halloween cowboy costume.

Grant walked over the berm on the opposite side of the compound from McCabe and began his first watch at the perimeter.

***

After several hours, Janaina called Grant and McCabe over. She stared at the pistol hanging at Grant's side.

"I've been trusted with adult toys," Grant said.

"I am half relieved," Janaina said, "and half terrified."

"That makes two of us."

She led them both back to Dixit's work area.

"I have completed the analysis of the white larva," Dixit said.

McCabe put his hands together in mock prayer. "Please tell me it isn't from a giant fly."

"Most certainly not," Dixit said. "It is an immature form of the pterosaur."

"That can't be right," Grant said.

Dixit pointed to two identical charts on his tablet. "The DNA, it is an exact match."

"There are similar examples in nature," Janaina said. "Parasitic wasps lay eggs in crickets. The larvae mature within the cricket before driving it to its death."

"A pterosaur isn't a wasp. But that idea might explain…"

Grant pulled what was left of the pterosaur carcass out of the cooler by the table. He examined the tip of the bill. Gripping the bill with one hand, with the other he probed the hole on the end of the bill with a finger. He pulled and extended a bone tube from the lower bill.

"That would be the ovipositor," Janaina said. "The pterosaur could fly over an ant, hover over its head, and then with one snap down, the egg is inserted through a hole small enough to heal over."

"And when the larva matures?" McCabe asked.

"It pops out of the ant's head like a jack-in-the-box," Janaina said. "At the ant's expense."

"How does the ant manage with this thing in its head?"

"An intruder like this is generally benign. If it killed the ant too early, it wouldn't have time to mature. Some of them even control the host, like the parasitic wasps do."

"Larvae maturing inside ants," Grant said, "would mean that pterosaurs would not need nests, an evolutionary advantage in a place where an ankylosaur might wander by and devour the eggs."

"And that explains the size of the ants," Janaina added. "Larger ants carry the larvae to a larger size, and live long enough to reproduce other ants."

"Great little science class, kids," McCabe said. "But what good does knowing all that crap do us?"

"It means that one poison will kill both a larvae and a pterosaur," Dixit said. "And the same genetic similarity that keeps ant antibodies from attacking the larvae means that the ant is vulnerable as well."

"You'll mix us up an all-purpose killer?" McCabe said.

"Excepting humans of course?" Grant added.

"In the same way that you can spray a garden plant, kill the insects, and still eat the fruit. I have isolated a genetic weakness the animals on the plateau have that we do not."

"Then get mixing," McCabe said. "The next attack may come at any time." McCabe made a beeline for Griggs to share the news.

Dixit opened a big box and began to rifle through tubes of liquid chemicals. Grant bent his head to Janaina's ear.

"Can I have a minute with Dixit?" he whispered.

"Yes," she said. "As long as you are saving me from shaming you into making an apology."

Grant stepped over to Dixit. Dixit pointedly did not look up from the sample box.

"Say." Grant paused as he realized he didn't remember Dixit's first name, which made him feel even worse. "I am so sorry for embarrassing you into going out to the Bobcat. If I'd have just gone, Katsoros wouldn't have felt like she needed to go with you, she'd be alive, and you would have avoided a near-death experience. With only one person down there, the ankylosaur might not have even attacked. I feel like hell, and there's no way to make it up to you, but I want you to know that I wish that I could."

Dixit turned and looked Grant in the eye. Grant expected to see fury. Instead he saw sorrow.

"Your frustration was quite warranted," Dixit said. "I must have appeared such a coward. I wanted to go on each expedition, to gather my own samples. But Ms. Katsoros would not permit it. Her orders kept me here doing the science, covering up all the secrets. I have a sick mother, and great debts, and that gives Transworld mighty leverage over my actions."

Now Grant felt even worse about acting like a jerk. He could barely meet Dixit's gaze.

"I should have found a way to tell you," Dixit continued. "To tell everyone. Perhaps in that way I am the coward after all."

"Not in the least."

"And you may feel remorse at Ms. Katsoros's death. Do not. You did not know her as I did. She was an evil woman. And while she promised all would return from this expedition, I have no doubt she would have left here to their death anyone who did not promise silence. And she did not trust you at all."

The tension in Grant's neck eased as a bit of his guilt slipped away.

"That helps. But Dorothy still felt bad melting the Wicked Witch."

"Come again?"

Grant realized they didn't share the same cultural touchstones. "Never mind."

"Also, permit me to apologize to you for my initial rudeness. You have proven yourself to be a true man of science."

Grant shook Dixit's hand. "Find us the right poison. Who knows when the next animal attack will come."

Suddenly, the scream of a pterosaur ripped through the air overhead.

CHAPTER TWENTY-ONE

High above, the sun backlit five pterosaurs in a tight V formation. They tucked their wings to their sides and dove. In unison, they let loose a chorused shriek.

"Get cover!" McCabe shouted. He fired a burst from his rifle at the pterosaurs. Bullets passed through the formation. The pterosaurs stayed on target for the container.

Dixit dropped his tablet and ran for the sleeping container. Janaina and Grant were right behind him. Just as Dixit got to the doors, Riffaud burst out in a t-shirt and boxer shorts, rifle at the ready.

Up on the berm, Griggs sent a spray of bullets at the diving dinosaurs. The formation flicked around them and the bullets flew by.

Dixit and Janaina jumped into the container. Grant remembered the pistol that beat against his hip with every step. He drew it and stood in the container doorway, knowing that he was halfway between heroic and ridiculous, ready to fend off a dinosaur attack with a revolver.

Riffaud stood beside McCabe. They aimed skyward and fired. Tracers lanced the air. Griggs joined in from the berm, laying down a leading edge of lead across the pterosaurs' paths.

The dinosaurs' wings snapped out to full extension. As if all one, the group wheeled left and climbed. They shrieked and it sent a chill up Grant's spine. The dinosaurs crossed the compound's edge and turned to make another pass. The flock screamed in time with every beat of their wings.

"Track the noisy bastards as they come in," McCabe ordered. "Open up at four hundred meters."

The pterosaurs turned toward the compound, then dove in again. The three soldiers kept their weapons aimed at the dinosaurs, with fingers ready against the triggers.

A split second before the pterosaurs came into range, a sixth one rocketed in from the north at ground level. Its bill skewered Griggs through the back and plucked him off the berm. With a snap of its head it threw Griggs's body at McCabe's feet, and then zipped over the far berm. The pterosaurs above scattered and broke off the attack.

That made no sense to Grant. The pterosaurs had the advantage in numbers, had sidelined Griggs. Why break off now?

The earth under his feet shuddered. Then the sleeping container flew up into the air. One door swung open and backhanded Grant to the ground. The container landed on its side with a crash and the center buckled like a sheet of aluminum foil.

A giant soldier ant's head protruded from a hole where the container had been. It snapped its mandibles together and scrambled above ground.

Beside McCabe and Riffaud, two more ants burst from the ground. McCabe whirled just in time to jam the barrel of his rifle between the ant's spread mandibles and fire. Bullets ripped the ant's head in half and it sprayed reddish ooze all over McCabe. Its momentum carried the rest of the ant forward and it pinned McCabe to the ground.

The second ant lunged for Riffaud. He dodged left and sent a spray of bullets into the creature's side. Rounds rippled along the ant's three segments and the impact drove it on its side. Six legs jerked in death throes as the body shuddered.

Janaina and Dixit crawled out of the damaged container's open door. Slick, bright blood plastered Dixit's hair to the side of his head.

A second ant crawled out of the hole near Grant. He rolled over on his stomach and aimed at the ant's center segment. He fired and hit it dead on. The ant didn't flinch.

The two ants charged after Janaina and Dixit. Grant fired again and the shot went wide.

Another ant launched itself from the hole. Riffaud dropped his rifle to his hip and fired on automatic. Ant legs snapped as the bullets grazed the earth. The ant dropped to the ground. Its stubs flailed in the air and the mandibles snapped in frustration in Riffaud's direction.

The ants hunting Janaina and Dixit closed within meters. Grant aimed with both hands and pumped two rounds into the head of one ant. It staggered and paused.

Riffaud turned and sent another burst of rounds into the other ant. Reddish ooze exploded from cracks in its exoskeleton.

A sixth ant sprang from the hole behind Riffaud. The ant lunged. Its mandibles clamped Riffaud's arms to his sides at his waist. The ant lifted him with the slightest movement of its head and squeezed. Riffaud cried out and his rifle clattered to the ground.

The ant Grant had wounded grabbed Dixit by the ankles in its mandibles and pulled. Dixit hit the ground hard, face-first. The second ant scurried past and clamped on Janaina. It lifted her off the ground like plucking a flower.

The ant carrying Riffaud turned and retreated down the hole. Riffaud's head slammed into the top of the tube and he went limp. The ant carrying Janaina headed for the same hole.

Grant took aim at the second ant's head, conflicted at stopping the creature and risking shooting Janaina. He re-aimed at the ant's last segment. He pulled the trigger.

The ant carrying Dixit sprinted ahead. It blocked the shot and Grant's bullet pierced the ant's head. The ant dropped Dixit and crashed on its side.

Janaina's ant disappeared underground. Her scream echoed from the hole in the earth. She already sounded a hundred miles away.

CHAPTER TWENTY-TWO

Grant cursed himself for not firing the pistol sooner, better, faster. He raised himself off the ground and went to Dixit. Dixit lay face down, still. Grant rolled him over.

Wide, white eyes darted back and forth. His hands and feet shook, but the rest of his body stayed rigid. He wasn't bleeding, nothing looked broken. He was in some kind of shock. And understandably so.

"Dixit. It's dead. You're okay. Everything's going to be fine." He gave him a shake. "Dixit!"

Dixit's eyes focused on Grant. "I'm alive?"

"And uninjured. Somehow."

Grant went over to McCabe. He didn't move. The ant carcass looked to have crushed him.

McCabe opened his eyes. He gritted his teeth in pain as he inhaled. "Get this damn thing off me."

Grant laid his hands against the ant carcass. It felt surprisingly cold, and smooth as a polished sea shell. He dug in his heels and pushed. The thing didn't move.

McCabe closed his eyes. "Damn it."

Grant saw Riffaud's rifle on the ground. He picked it up and pointed it at McCabe's midsection. McCabe opened his eyes.

"What the hell are you doing?"

Grant thrust the rifle barrel down at McCabe. It crossed over his stomach, under the ant and into the ground. Grant squatted, grabbed the buttstock with both hands, grunted, and heaved. Muscles in his back stretched like harp strings. But just when he feared they were about to break, the ant rolled off of McCabe. Grant leaned against the rifle and looked down at McCabe with a satisfied smile.

"Thanks," McCabe said.

Then he grabbed the rifle with both hands and yanked it out of Grant's grasp. He smacked Grant in the chest with the buttstock and sent him staggering back.

"And don't ever use a firearm for something that stupid again." McCabe sat up and moaned in pain. He ran a hand along his side. "Damn ant broke my rib."

Grant offered him a hand up. McCabe gave him a derisive look and used the ant carcass as a support instead. He walked over and checked Griggs, but the gaping hole in his body left no doubt that he was dead. McCabe looked over at Dixit, who'd transitioned to sitting up.

"Is he okay?" McCabe said.

"Shaken, but not hurt from what I can see."

McCabe picked up his rifle, dropped the magazine, counted rounds and reloaded. "Did you see those bastards? Coordinated attack. Flying dinos distracted us then the ants came up from below."

"Seriously?"

"I've been in combat since I was eighteen. I know tactics when I see it. The dinos aren't afraid of us—the attack in the jungle proved that. And they had more of an advantage here, coming fast from above. They could have dived in and shredded us."

"They did attack Griggs."

"Because he was the only one on high ground, the only one the ants couldn't burrow underneath and surprise. The dinos wanted the ants taking the risk to kill us."

"But they didn't kill us. They took Riffaud and Janaina alive, tried to take Dixit as well. If they wanted them dead I'm betting those mandibles could have cut them in two. We saw them do the same thing with phoberomys at the bridge. Taking prey alive."

McCabe stepped toward the hole in the ground. "Then I'd better go get Riffaud while he still is."

"And Janaina," Grant reminded him. "But alone against who knows how many ants at the other end of that tunnel? You'll end up dead."

McCabe raised his rifle across his chest. "I only need to get through enough of them to rescue Riffaud."

"What if instead we can get through all of them?" Grant turned to Dixit. "How close are you to perfecting that poison?"

"The formula is untested, but I am certain that it will work, even at low dosages with external contact."

"You expect me to bet my life on that shaky endorsement?" McCabe said.

Grant waved McCabe off. "Dixit, how much can you make?"

"Four, perhaps six liters with the components we have on hand."

"How fast will it kill?"

"Seconds, perhaps."

"That's a damn long time to be staring down a charging ant," McCabe said.

"You'd have to stare the ant down longer without it," Grant said.

"It still falls upon us to deliver the poison," Dixit said.

"Yeah, where's an aerial tanker when you need one?" Grant said. "We could spray it all over them."

"We still could," McCabe said. "We could use a chaff tube. Coat all the chaff with the poison. Light it. Boom. Everything that touches some of that confetti dies."

"That would work," Dixit said.

"The colony will be underground," Grant said. "We can't fire chaff over it. We'll need to go into it, find Janaina and Riffaud, and get out."

"You take care of the poison," McCabe said. "I'll take care of the delivery system."

Grant had an idea about how to sneak the three of them in and out of the colony alive. They weren't going to like how he was going to do it.

CHAPTER TWENTY-THREE

An hour later, Dixit had five liters of death split into two plastic containers. Grant felt guilty that they were about to destroy such scientific wonders. Though not guilty enough to sacrifice himself and Janaina to spare the murderous things.

McCabe arrived with the chaff tube. A strap tied off at both ends of the tube let him sling it over his shoulder. He'd salvaged a cell of the Bobcat's battery and wired it to the charge at the tube's base. The battery hung from his belt with the ignition switch from the Bobcat wired in as the on switch.

"Let's make this thing lethal," McCabe said.

He disconnected the wires and propped the tube straight up. With his knife he punched a series of holes in the lightweight cover at the tube's end. Dixit took one container and poured the poison through the holes. When he finished, McCabe picked up the tube and shook it like a maraca.

"Whoa," Grant said. "Is that safe?"

"Don't sweat it, Dino Doc. Nothing except electrical power to the igniter is going to set this off."

He and Dixit did the same procedure to a second tube and set it beside the tunnel entrance. "This one's the defensive weapon. If any survivors come charging out of the tube after us, boom, we blast them."

"There's still the problem of sneaking in," Grant said. "The first ant that sees us will send a chemical alarm and hundreds will scramble to the nest's defense. But I have a way around it."

He grabbed the antenna of a dead ant. Half the head was still attached. He dragged it over to the group.

"Ant eyesight is poor, not needed since they're underground so much. Janaina explained how the ants communicate with pheromones to let other ants know who they are or what is going on outside the nest. We're going to disguise ourselves as ants. With smell."

He scooped a handful of ant internals out of the ant's shell of a head. Then he spread the gooey mess all over his chest. The smell screwed straight into his sinuses and stayed there. His eyes watered.

"Preserve us, that is an awful smell," Dixit said.

"You sure that will work?" McCabe asked.

"During the attack, you were covered in ant blood by the first ant. The rest left you alone. You were pinned under the body, but still in plain sight and alive. I think the stink masked your own smell."

"Great," McCabe said. "We have poison that might kill, camouflage that might conceal, and a weapon that might fire. What could possibly go wrong?"

The three coated themselves in ant. By the time they'd finished, Grant's olfactory senses had dulled from the overload and he almost couldn't smell himself. Almost.

McCabe taped flashlights to the barrels of the three rifles. He handed one to Dixit and held the other out in front of Grant.

"Here's an upgrade," McCabe said. "I'll take back my pistol."

Grant traded him weapons. McCabe returned his holster to his hip.

"I must confess that I am wholly unfamiliar with firearms," Dixit said.

"Well, that's a shock," McCabe said. "We'll be in a tunnel. Point the weapon away from us and at the horde of ants. You'll hit something."

"Hopefully the poison will keep anything from being alive to chase us out," Grant said.

"Time's wasting," McCabe said. He slung a chaff tube across his back and connected the wires to the battery on his belt. "Let's roll."

Grant tucked a machete into his belt. Dixit had a short knife he'd found somewhere tucked into his. The three clicked on their flashlights and entered the tunnel. As the daylight receded, dread swelled up inside Grant. Memories of the cavern in Montana flashed by.

"When I get out of here," he said to himself. "I'm not even going to take a subway again."

The tunnel had standing room in the center. The ants had scoured away an almost perfect tube, large enough that two could pass each other with both carrying something. That gave Grant more hope. After seeing Riffaud knocked unconscious, he was afraid the trip in might have killed Janaina outright. The walls glistened with the saliva the ants had used to seal the earth in place. A damp, peaty smell wafted up from deeper down the tunnel.

They continued on for a while.

"Not that I am in favor of it," Dixit said, "but shouldn't we have encountered an ant by now?"

"Maybe this tunnel was specifically dug for the attack on us, and has no other purpose," Grant said.

After a few minutes more, they came to a fork in the tunnel.

"Now which path do we select?" Dixit said.

McCabe checked a compass. "We've been heading west. We keep heading west. Any nest would be closer to the center of the plateau."

"I agree," Grant said. Being able to plumb Janaina's well of expertise on ant behavior would have been more than welcome right now.

McCabe pulled his knife and etched an arrow into the wall at the tunnel junction. It pointed back to the entrance. "We may need to find our way out in a hurry."

"Don't tell me you've read *Journey to the Center of the Earth*?" Grant said.

"A favorite when I was a kid." McCabe passed by Grant and tapped him twice on the chest with the side of the knife blade. "And your book totally ripped off Jules Verne."

Grant swallowed his reply that Jules Verne hadn't nearly died researching his book the way Grant had.

"Do me a favor," Grant said. "When we get back, don't leave a review."

McCabe sheathed his knife and pushed ahead down the tunnel.

Minutes later, a scraping noise from far ahead broke the silence. McCabe snapped his flashlight to high power and sent the beam down the tunnel's center.

The ruby red head of an advancing soldier ant lit up like a neon sign. McCabe doused his flashlight.

"Kill the lights," he whispered. "We're about to see if your camouflage works, Dino Doc."

Grant and Dixit cut off their lights. The darkness in the tunnel was absolute. Grant fought back a feeling of claustrophobia, as if without light to keep them at bay, the tunnel walls would close in and suffocate him.

The ant's scratching grew closer. Then there was a regular measured hiss, an exhalation. Grant would have been thrilled at the discovery of active respiration in an insect if the insect hadn't been centimeters from being able to kill him.

Scratching reached the far wall and stopped. The sharp smell of uric acid prickled Grant's nose. Grant pressed his back harder into the tunnel wall. Something hard and cold touched his arm. He flinched and stifled a scream. The thing ran down his blood-camouflaged arm and over his hand. He recognized the feel from earlier in the day. It was the ant's antenna. He was being scanned.

The antenna ran across his chest and toward Dixit. It touched Dixit and he yelped. Grant clamped a hand over Dixit's mouth.

"It will kill intruders," Grant whispered in Dixit's ear.

The antenna made another pass over Grant's chest. Then the leg scratches restarted, passed them, and continued down the tunnel. When they were nearly imperceptible, Grant exhaled and took his hand from Dixit's mouth. Dixit immediately doubled over and threw up.

"Looks like we passed the sniff test, Doc," McCabe said.

"Never doubted we would," Grant lied.

Now that his eyes had adapted to the utter darkness, he realized that it wasn't as complete as he'd first thought. The far end of the tunnel was lighter. "Is it my imagination, or is there daylight down there?"

"Let's find out." McCabe alone turned on his flashlight and the three made their way down the tunnel.

They rounded a corner and came to another intersection. But the branch tunnel here headed up a steep incline to the surface. Daylight shined through the hole like a fuzzy spotlight.

"We were still going west?" Grant asked.

"Plus or minus five degrees all the way," McCabe said.

"Then this tunnel comes up somewhere other than our compound. It might be where Janaina and Riffaud are."

"One way to know," McCabe said and he headed up the offshoot tunnel.

The others followed. The last few yards were practically vertical.

"Let's climb!" McCabe said.

The three began to hack out handholds in the hardened earth.

A puff of wind blew down the tunnel. It brought a rank smell that Grant remembered from the crash site and the compound. It gave him a chill.

The air ahead stank of pterosaur.

CHAPTER TWENTY-FOUR

The ant tunnel exited among several large bushes. The three men crawled out and took cover in the branches.

Before them rose the high ground at the western edge of the plateau. The bottom dozen meters were a sheer, stone cliff face. Above that, the barren, brown earth rose more gradually. Holes about two meters wide pockmarked the hillside. Excavated earth, rocks, and bits of debris lay before each hole.

"I have a bad feeling about what lives in those holes," Grant said.

As if on cue, a pterosaur waddled out of one little cave. It turned around and scratched some dirt out through the entrance. The earth splattered on some of the debris. The pterosaur walked out, picked up the scrap and shook it clean. It returned the piece to the ground and nudged it back into the same location.

"I recognize those parts," McCabe said. "They're from the C-130."

"Why would the pterosaurs do that?" Dixit said.

"Bowerbirds do the same thing," Grant said. "Decorating nests to attract mates. All the glass and metal on the plane would have been something new and exciting. Now it makes more sense that they took the radio we tried to salvage. For its decorative, rather than functional, purposes."

Two pterosaurs flew into separate holes. A third emerged and took flight.

"We'd last about a second out there before those things spotted us and attacked," McCabe said.

"Look over to the left," Dixit said.

At the edge of the cliff carcasses of dead ants littered the ground like cars in a junk yard. All the heads had exploded.

"Looks like the aftermath of an epic ant/pterosaur battle," McCabe said.

"No," Grant said. "I'll bet that's where the larvae direct the ants to go before they emerge. They drive the ant closer to the pterosaur rookery."

Scratching sounded from the tunnel, followed by a stifled squeal. Grant's heart jumped and he flattened himself against the ground.

A soldier ant crawled past them. It gripped a plump, furry phoberomys in its mandibles. Spider webbing, like the fibers used on the ant bridge, wrapped the struggling creature. The ant approached the base of the cliff and dropped the phoberomys amidst a group of shriveled lumps.

As the ant retreated, a series of pterosaur cries sounded from within the tiny caves. Two emerged and launched. They tucked into steep dives toward the phoberomys. At the last moment, they flared their wings like parachutes and braked centimeters from the ground on either side of the phoberomys.

Both pterosaurs screamed and entered into a violent duel. Like two fencers, they used their bills as rapiers, jabbing, parrying. Wings spread for balance, they slashed at each other as the terrified phoberomys rocked at their feet. Finally, the larger of the two scored a hit with a slice across its opponent's chest. The victim screeched and retreated. Blood seeped from the wound. It launched and flew back up to its lair.

The victor pierced the phoberomys sack with its bill and the little mammal squealed. Then the pterosaur carried its prey back up to its cave. It dropped it at the entrance. Two smaller pterosaurs scrambled out of the cave into the daylight and began to tear shreds from their mother's offering.

"The ants are feeding the pterosaurs?" Dixit said.

"The larvae in their brains," Grant said. "They must take over and make the ant colony support the pterosaurs. That was what they were doing bringing phoberomys over the ant bridge that day. They secure them with webbing then deliver them alive to the colony."

The baby pterosaurs returned to their cave. The mother flung the web-covered phoberomys carcass over the edge. It handed with the rest at the base of the cliff.

An awful thought crossed Grant's mind. "Which is why they took Janaina and Riffaud instead of killing them."

"Then we'd damn well better get back in that hole and find them," McCabe said. "Before they turn into tonight's dinner."

CHAPTER TWENTY-FIVE.

McCabe marked the trail with another reversed arrow and led them west. The increased pace took a toll. Heavier breathing appeared to make his broken rib more painful, and Grant caught him red-faced, fighting back pain.

"You need a break," Grant said. "Before you pass out."

"Riffaud might be seconds from death. He's not dying because we're late."

They passed two ants heading in the opposite direction. Other than a fleeting swipe with their antennae, they seemed to take no notice of the three, even with the lit flashlights. Grant wondered how long the stink he'd rubbed into their clothes would last.

Light appeared up ahead. Soon the tunnel forked and dead ended at two different rooms. A low thrum of scratching and hissing came from the first, darker room. McCabe motioned them all to crouch down near the entrance.

McCabe played his flashlight inside. The beam landed on a seething mass of ants. Worker ants, the smaller versions without the soldier's mandibles, like the ones that had made the bridge, moved in all directions at once, and pulsed like a living carpet. Some carried smaller, squirming pupae.

"The center of the colony," Grant whispered. "The nursery. Somewhere in there is the queen."

"And Riffaud?"

"Not down there."

They backtracked and chose the other fork. It opened to a smaller chamber. Holes in the ceiling acted like skylights. Other tunnels led deeper into the colony. Several worker ants crawled up the walls and across the ceiling. In the center of the room hung over a dozen webbed cocoons, just like the one they'd seen delivered to the pterosaur colony. Between them all hung two much larger versions, two meters long.

"That's them." McCabe said.

He took aim at an ant closest to the cocoons. Grant pushed down the barrel of McCabe's rifle.

"Fire that thing and those ants will panic. They'll scatter all the cocoons for safety and we'll never find them."

"Then what's your plan?"

Grant paused. "Ants are specialized. These here just care for the cocoons until they're delivered. If we free a bunch of phoberomys, the ants will chase them down. While they're distracted, we get Janaina and Riffaud and get the hell out of here."

McCabe shouldered his rifle opposite of the poisoned chaff container. The sling touched his ribs and he sucked in a sharp, pained breath. He exhaled slowly and then drew his knife. "Good a plan as any. Dixit, you ready?"

Dixit lay down his rifle and drew his knife. "Most certainly. Especially the 'get the hell out of here' part."

Grant slung his rifle and drew his machete. The big blade was a little overkill, and he'd have to be careful cutting Janaina free with it. "Let's go."

They paused while a worker ant scuttled by. Then they entered the chamber.

The three split and went to different cocoons. In unison they each sliced one from the ceiling. Grant's hit the ground with a thud. The phoberomys inside wriggled. Grant knelt and grabbed the webbing. He stretched it up and then sliced through it. With a yank he pulled the cocoon apart. It made a sound like tearing cardboard. The phoberomys shook itself as if waking from a horrible dream. Then it bolted for one of the exit tunnels. A split second later, McCabe's and Dixit's phoberomys raced for a different exit.

One escapee grazed the leg of an ant. The ant stiffened, and then whipped its antennae around fast enough to touch the phoberomys as it slipped away into the darkness. The ant shuddered, no doubt passing some combination of physical and chemical alert to the other ants. In response, a second ant sprinted down the tunnel after the phoberomys. The first ant followed.

The trick worked. The three men began to slash and free phoberomys as fast as they could manage. Each one set off a panic as it contacted worker ants. One raced around the chamber's edge, unable to find an escape, and leaving a hurricane of frantic ants following its trail. It finally stumbled upon an exit and led the remaining ants out, which left the chamber clear.

Dixit raised his arms to cut free another phoberomys. His shirt caught on a protruding rock and tore straight up the back. He chopped the creature free anyway.

Grant cut loose one more phoberomys and then moved to support Riffaud as McCabe cut him free. Grant lowered Riffaud to the ground and McCabe slashed the cocoon open. The stench of death rose from the webbing.

Riffaud's skin was the color of slate. Lifeless eyes stared from under half-shut lids. A helmet of dried blood caked his hair where he'd struck the tunnel after his capture. Grant hoped his death had been blessedly instantaneous.

"Damn it to hell," McCabe said. He hung his head.

Grant shook McCabe's shoulder. "Janaina! She may still be alive."

Grant stepped sideways and grabbed Janaina's cocoon. McCabe freed her with a savage slash, his face red with rage. Grant lowered Janaina to the ground. He beat back the urge to chop at the possibly suffocating webbing out of fear of hurting her. He tucked the blade in sideways and ran it down the cocoon like he was cutting the wrapping around a priceless vase. He peeled back the webbing.

Janaina lay still. Grant's heart sank. He bowed his head.

Janaina's eyes flickered open. She sucked in a deep breath and snapped upright. Her chest smacked Grant in the head, and he went sprawling.

"You're alive," Dixit said.

"Where am I?" she said. She looked around the chamber. "I was outside, there was an ant…"

"Don't worry about that now," McCabe said. "We need to get you out of here."

Janaina looked down at Grant. "What are you doing lying on the ground?"

Grant rose to his knees. "Rescuing you, obviously."

Janaina looked at Riffaud's corpse. "*Ai, meu Deus.*"

"Can you walk?" Grant said as he stood up.

With his help, she rose to her feet. "Pins and needles for a minute." She shook her legs. Grant draped her arm across his shoulder and led her toward the exit tunnel.

One of the ants crawled back into the chamber with a captured phoberomys in its mouth. Its antennae passed along Dixit's bare back. He screamed in surprise. The ant dropped the phoberomys which scampered back down the tunnel. The ant made a hissing noise and began to shudder.

"Damn it," McCabe said. "It touched your bare skin. Run!"

McCabe jabbed the barrel of his rifle against the ant's head and fired. The blast echoed in the tiny room. The ant's head vaporized and the remaining segments backpedaled down the other tunnel.

Grant knew that if the worker ant's pheromone release and vibrating signal hadn't warned the colony of intruders, then that gunshot certainly had. They'd be lucky to make it out of the colony alive.

"We need to run," he said to Janaina. "Can you?"

She lifted herself from his shoulder. "I'd better." She took two hesitant steps, then accelerated into a sprint.

Dixit came running out of the chamber next. In his panic he hadn't even picked up his rifle.

Just as he passed the fork to the colony's main nest, a soldier ant thrust its head from the darkness. Its red mandibles yawned wide open. They bracketed Dixit's waist and clamped shut. Dixit screamed and the ant yanked him back down the darkened tunnel. Something crunched and Dixit fell silent.

McCabe rushed out of the chamber. A soldier ant crawled right behind him. It snapped its mandibles at his leg, but only grazed him. That was enough.

McCabe dropped to the ground. He whirled and fired a salvo of shots into the creature. Bullets shattered multiple segments and the creature fell dead. Then McCabe blasted away at the tunnel ceiling on full automatic. The roof disintegrated into a cloud of dirt, then the tunnel back to the chamber collapsed around the dead ant.

Grant lifted McCabe up under the shoulders. The gash in his leg exposed bone. Grant winced.

"Collapse that tunnel to the nest," Grant said. "And we'll get the hell out of here."

McCabe looked at the wound on his leg. He shook his head. "I'm not going anywhere. You go. I'll buy you time."

"You can't hold off the whole colony."

"I won't have to." McCabe unslung the chaff tube from his shoulder. "I'm going to kill them."

"The poison isn't instant. They'll tear you apart before they die."

"But they'll still die. They're going to pay for Riffaud and Griggs."

Grant was about to raise another objection when McCabe let a burst of rounds loose into advancing ants in the tunnel. Ant parts splattered the wall.

"Get out of here. Save Janaina and yourself. I'll be pissed as hell if I die in here for nothing."

Grant couldn't argue. "Good luck."

"Losers need luck."

Grant backed down the tunnel. McCabe checked the switch for the chaff and slung the tube loose at his shoulder. He stood and steadied himself against the wall, then pointed his rifle down toward the nest with one hand, the chaff dispenser with the other. Arm muscles bulged as he pulled the trigger and sprayed bullets into the tube ahead of him.

"What's the matter, boys? Allergic to lead?" McCabe staggered out of sight. "Payback's coming!"

More automatic weapons fire sounded. Muzzle flashes flickered in the darkness. Grant turned and ran for the exit.

Behind him an explosion rocked the walls as McCabe fired off the chaff tube. His sharp scream followed, then silence.

From far ahead came the low glow of light at the tunnel entrance. Janaina's shadow played back and forth across it as she ran.

Scraping sounded behind him, coming up fast. Grant turned to see two ants charging, their heads and mandibles filling the tunnel. He sprayed a half dozen rounds their way. The ants didn't stop. Grant sprinted for his life.

Up ahead, Janaina broke out into daylight. But that end of the tunnel seemed impossibly far away. He could smell, no, he could *sense* that the ants were right behind him. His heart slammed in his chest and his leg muscles burned like they were on fire.

A crash sounded centimeters behind him. Then another. He looked over his shoulder. The ants lay in a pile. He stopped running and looked closer, amazed that his un-aimed shots had hit them somewhere vital.

They hadn't. The ants were in one piece. Except for the strips of aluminum foil plastered to their bodies.

The poison had worked.

Grant staggered to the tunnel exit, completely out of breath and nearly dragging the rifle. He stepped into the daylight. Janaina was waiting.

"McCabe? Dixit?" she asked.

Grant shook his head. "Didn't make it. But McCabe blew the poison into the nest. Any ants that aren't already dead soon will be. We're safe."

Her eyes widened. "No we're not." She pointed over Grant's shoulder.

Out to the west, by the pterosaur rookery, a dark cloud appeared to rise into the air.

Even at this distance, it looked angry.

CHAPTER TWENTY-SIX

"Back in the tunnel?" Janaina asked.

"Blocked by dead ants by now. And those pterosaurs will walk in to find us, the way they did at the plane wreck."

"And the jungle won't hide us."

The toppled sleeping container lay in the compound's center

"The sleeping container," Grant said "We can close the doors behind us."

"It's a cage. How long can we survive in there?"

Grant handed her his rifle. "Longer than out here."

From the west, the pterosaurs were closing fast. Janaina ran for the container. Grant noticed the second chaff tube beside the tunnel entrance. He grabbed it and followed.

The container's right door hung down to cut the opening in half. They ducked under as they dashed in. Pterosaur screeches sounded overhead. Grant reached down to pull the left door up into place. It didn't budge.

"Damn. The hinge must be bent or something."

Janaina joined him and they gave the door a yank. The hinges moaned and the door swung closed. They secured it from the inside.

"Maybe they won't know we're in here," Grant said.

"They saw us go in and can smell us from the outside."

"Forgive my wishful thinking."

Pterosaurs screamed from just outside the container. Metal crunched as creatures landed on the container's top facing side.

"Maybe they'll get frustrated and leave," Grant said. "Or do you want to shoot down that bit of optimism as well?"

"No, you go ahead and nurture that one."

Claws scraped like knife blades against the metal door. It jerked against the hinges as a pterosaur tried to open it. The lock held.

"See," Grant said. "They can't get in."

Suddenly a bill pierced through the top of the container. It missed Grant by millimeters. He jumped back.

Janaina jammed the rifle barrel against the container next to the bill and fired. A pterosaur screamed and the bill withdrew. Another bill slammed through the container at the far end. Other bills hammered at the container from all sides, leaving dents in the steel.

"Limited ammunition," she said. "Unlimited dinosaurs."

Grant smiled and hefted the chaff tube. "But we have this."

Janaina grabbed the two wires hanging from the bottom and held them up. "And?"

Grant realized that the ignition system for the tube was still strapped to McCabe somewhere in the dying ant nest. "McCabe said only electricity could set it off."

A bill smashed through the vertical wooden floor of the container and into one of the sleeping seats. The bill stuck and the pterosaur jerked the seat back and forth trying to free it. The seat tore loose, and its weight snapped the bill in two. The chair dropped to the ground and the jagged stump of the pterosaur bill slipped away.

Grant and Janaina began a frantic search through the mess in the container for something, anything with a battery. Grant remembered the flashlight on the rifle.

"Got it!" He slit the securing duct tape with his machete. He flicked the switch. The bulb glowed. He turned it off.

Another bill pierced the weak spot along the crease in the container. A second punched in beside it. Then a third.

"They are working together," Janaina said. "Opening a hole to get in."

"We'll use that hole to get this out."

He rolled the chaff tube on its side. He unscrewed the flashlight and tied the two chaff tube wires off to contacts inside.

"Is that enough power to light the charge?" Janaina said.

"I have no idea, and no other options."

"And this poison will kill the pterosaurs?"

"Same answer."

Two more bills speared the container top and disappeared.

"As soon as there's a hole the size of this tube," Grant said, "I'm going to jam the tube through it. Then you need to throw that flashlight switch."

"Roger that." She nodded in satisfaction. "I decided I'm keeping that phrase."

She gripped the flashlight in both hands and stared at the top of the container.

Pterosaurs pounded on all sides. Janaina shouted something but it was lost in the din. Bills pierced the top faster and faster. Several peppered the middle section until the perforations nearly all touched.

Suddenly a pterosaur head burst through the weakened steel. It screamed and with a snap of its head it slammed Grant into the side of the container.

Janaina dropped the flashlight and grabbed the rifle. The pterosaur shrieked at her. She jammed the rifle up into its open bill and fired. The bullet blasted through the elongated rear of the dinosaur's skull. Blood and brains splattered Grant's face.

The dinosaur dropped in through the hole and fell at Grant's feet. Grant grabbed the chaff tube and shoved it up through the hole in the container. "Hit it!"

Janaina dropped the rifle and scrambled for the flashlight. It lay in a pool of pterosaur blood. She grabbed for it and it slipped through her fingers.

Enraged pterosaurs accelerated the assault. Bills pierced all sides of the container. Pterosaurs pulled at the door and it bent in the hinges.

Janaina dove into the dinosaur blood with both hands. She gripped the flashlight, felt the switch, and pushed it.

Grant braced for the explosion. The chaff tube boomed. The recoil tore the tube from his hands. Grant looked through the hole in the roof to see a snowfall of flashing chaff flutter through and around a flock of soaring pterosaurs.

At the report of the chaff tube, the attack stopped.

Then the pterosaurs erupted in a chorused roar. The attack resumed, more furious than before.

Bills shredded the container sides. Grant shoved the tube into the ceiling hole to block another pterosaur invasion. Pterosaurs jabbed it from above so hard that it shoved Grant across the blood-soaked floor.

Dozens of pterosaur strikes dimpled the walls. A bill drove through the side and slashed Grant's arm. He dropped the chaff tube and clamped a hand to his bleeding bicep.

The container door bent outward in the middle and snapped off its hinges. Daylight flooded the interior and Grant squinted.

Janaina grabbed the rifle and pointed it at the open container door. Grant drew his machete and prepared to die.

The attack stopped. All around the container dying pterosaurs thudded to the ground. Through the open door, two hit the ground nearby and disappeared in a cloud of dust. Then all went silent.

"Could it be?" Janaina said.

She headed out the door, rifle pointed straight ahead. Grant followed her and they both stood in the compound's center.

"Well, I'm still not dead," Grant said. "But they are."

Dead pterosaurs littered the ground. Here and there a wing fluttered in the last spasms of the animal's death throes. To the west, a flock of pterosaurs retreated home. Some dropped out of formation and plummeted to the ground.

"They're going to take that poisoned chaff back to the rookery and kill the rest, aren't they?" Janaina said.

"Even if they don't, they're doomed. Some may be able to survive without the ants providing food, but with no way to gestate their larvae, this will be their last generation. I'd feel pretty melancholy about it if the damn things hadn't been trying to kill us."

"Transworld Union gets their way. No species to get in the way of mining uranium."

"We don't know that. We haven't seen the entire plateau. And when we get back, the whole world will know about this place."

The faint drone of aircraft engines came from far away. Grant and Janaina turned around to face east.

In the distance, the silhouette of a C-130 popped in and out of clouds. It banked left to head for the plateau.

"The chaff is gone," Janaina said. "They'll never see us."

"We need to make certain they do."

They began to search through the wreckage of the camp, pulling dead pterosaurs off smashed boxes and upturned crates. Grant hoped for a radio, a mirror, a flamethrower, anything that might cause a commotion pilots might notice from thousands of feet up. He pulled one box aside and revealed one of the big white parachutes from their initial drop.

"Here! Grab this."

He and Janaina dragged it out to an open area. Working from both ends, they untangled the sheet from itself and stretched it out. The plane popped out of a cloud on a course closer to the compound.

"Yes!" Janaina jumped and began to raise and lower the parachute.

Grant matched her movements and the parachute rose and fell like a great, white wave. Sunlight flickered off the metal fittings. His hope began to rise. They were going to get the hell out of here after all.

The C-130 leveled out, still over a kilometer from where they stood, and not coming any closer.

"No, no, no," Grant said. "Hey, over here!"

"Turn this way!" Janaina screamed.

They shouted, though there was no way the pilots could possibly hear them. Grant's arms ached as he flapped the parachute high over his head.

The plane continued on, turned left again, and headed away on a course to São Paulo. Clouds again swallowed it up.

Grant dropped the parachute. "That's it?" he yelled after the plane. "That's as hard as you're going to try?"

Janaina froze in shock and dropped her side of the parachute. A breeze picked up the edge, and the parachute blew across the compound.

Grant's heart sank to his knees. He was out of optimism. There was only so long they could survive in this land that so wanted to kill them.

CHAPTER TWENTY-SEVEN

"This isn't good," Grant said. "Who knows if Transworld will ever send another expedition out here, and if they do, when."

"Everything is a mess around the compound, but it isn't destroyed. We should be able to salvage much of the food, and the stream has fresh water."

"Eventually, we'll have to live off the land. And the truth is that we probably can't. These primitive plants are very simple. They won't have evolved deep reservoirs of nutrients and we won't be able to digest them. And I don't even want to think about eating phoberomys. Of course, all those problems will become academic if something out there eats us first." Grant pointed to the destroyed container. "And where would we live? That thing is more colander than container now."

"Then we must go home."

"There's no way up and out of here."

"Then we'll go down. If the indigenous people came up the cliff side to make those offerings, we should be able to go down."

"It's hundreds of feet, and I get scared on step ladders."

"More scared than facing dinosaurs?"

Grant paused. "Well, no. But even if we get to the bottom, what then? We're hundreds of miles from anything."

"But the river below will take us to the coast, or civilization long before that. I've spent months doing research in Amazonia. The world of the past is up here. That is your world. The jungle below, that is mine."

There was no hope of survival staying up here, and only a 90 percent chance that climbing down a cliff would give Grant a fatal heart attack. "Okay, I'm in."

Over the next half hour, they salvaged backpacks from the Swiss-cheesed container and stuffed them with food and water. Grant's rifle was the only firearm to be found and a check of his magazine showed only three rounds. Wherever McCabe had secured the rest of the ammunition, if there was any, was a mystery they didn't have time to solve. Janaina found two coils of rope and a second machete. That was all they had to get them back to São Paulo.

Grant checked all of Dixit's lab equipment. The combination of pterosaur and ant attacks had destroyed everything. Even the small laptop was in pieces. Grant smashed the case with the handle of his machete and extracted the hard drive. It might contain the only physical proof that anything up here had once existed.

The plateau's silence was even more unnerving with the pterosaur corpses surrounding them. The imperative to get away from all the death, human and animal, grew with each minute. By the time Grant shouldered his pack, the idea of climbing down the side of the plateau seemed like a relatively welcome relief.

The two of them scaled the berm around the compound for a final time and set out across the ankylosaur-churned ground around the perimeter. They followed the path they had beaten through the jungle that first day, when the plateau was still benign and they were excited about encountering a peaceful apatosaurus. The rifle slipped in Grant's sweating palms. Unlike his first walk along this route, he was hyper-aware that something new and deadly might raise its head at any moment.

At last the jungle opened up to the sacrificial clearing and the cliff face to the east. Below stretched a seemingly infinite green jungle, sliced by the blue-green water of the river that would take them home. Grant's sense of relief was tempered by dread about the next, literally large step he was about to take, off the side of a cliff. Janaina dropped her backpack beside a tree and Grant dropped his coil of rope beside it. They both stepped over to the edge.

The sheer drop seemed about twice as long as Grant remembered it. A jumble of boulders at the base promised an instant, gruesome death if he fell. His equilibrium did a little whirl and he stepped back away from the edge.

"Now, you can't be that way," Janaina said. She dropped her rope. "Remember that people climbed this with bare hands and feet."

"People younger. And thinner."

"I can see the path they have carved from here. We'll use this rope to get past this steep section where some of the foot holds look questionable. Then it will be, how you say, a walk in the park. Unlike climbing, gravity will do half the work."

"I'm afraid of gravity getting bossy and deciding to do all the work."

Janaina tied one of the coils of rope off to the trunk of the tree. Grant wandered over to the far end of the clearing, ostensibly to look again at the ankylosaur offerings the locals had erected, but in reality to relish the feeling of solid earth beneath his feet while he still could.

To the left, branches crashed. Suddenly, an ankylosaur burst into the clearing. Barely a hundred meters away, it was the same one they'd encountered before. Blood dried to black coated its neck. The knife still protruded from one eye socket and the other was just a scabby hollow. It bellowed with a bass roar that made the ground tremble.

In a panicked reaction, Grant leveled the rifle at the dinosaur and fired without aiming. The bullet ricocheted off the creature's back plating.

It might have been blind, but apparently it could still hear, smell, and feel. It turned its head in Grant's direction. Grant aimed and fired twice.

Both rounds deflected off the creature's cranial armor. It roared again and charged Grant. Out of bullets and ideas, he ran. He angled away from Janaina. He might die, but at least he'd give her time to get over the cliff. He dashed between two huge trees and into the jungle.

The ankylosaur rushed at full speed straight for Grant. Its head went between the two trees, but its body shell crashed hard into both. It squeaked as it jerked to a stop and its head smacked into the ground.

The thing was vulnerable, for a moment. Grant could finish it. He dropped the empty rifle and drew his machete. One thrust, through the eye socket and into its tiny brain. That was all it would take. He raised the blade with both hands.

"Hey dinosaur!" Janaina shouted. "Over here you big bully!"

In the clearing behind the animal, Janaina wound up and hurled a rock at the ankylosaur. It hit the creature in the leg. The animal roared and backed out of the two-tree trap. It turned to the sound of Janaina's voice.

"Yes, you!" She pegged it in the head with another rock. "Come see what picking on a woman gets you."

Grant grimaced. He'd cleared the way for Janaina's escape. Now they were both going to end up getting killed.

The dinosaur charged Janaina. She turned and ran back across the clearing, toward the cliff. She shouted again at the animal and it barreled toward her voice. It closed with each bound. Janaina approached the cliff's edge without slowing. Grant's heart skipped a beat. Could she stop?

The ankylosaur snapped at her heels. Janaina reached the edge of the cliff, shouted once more at the creature, and launched herself into the air.

"No!" Grant screamed.

Janaina disappeared over the edge. The blind ankylosaur careened over the precipice behind her. Too late, the animal realized its mistake as its front legs sailed out into space. It twisted to reverse course, but momentum dragged its rear legs across the earth, and it flew off the cliff. The great ball at the end of its tail smashed the ground as the animal rotated belly up and dropped toward the jungle below. Its diminishing scream followed it down and then cut off.

For a second Grant stood stunned at the sacrifice he'd just seen. Then he ran to the precipice. As he passed the tree he noticed that the rope that had been tied around the trunk was stretched out, tight and quivering over the edge of the cliff. He ran to the edge and looked down.

Janaina hung upside down, a loop of rope tied around one ankle. She looked up at Grant.

"You going to pull me up or just stand there gawking?"

Grant dropped his machete and pulled her up, hand over hand. Near the top, her hands found purchase and she turned herself upright and crawled up over the edge. She stood up and dusted some dirt from her shirt.

"What the hell did you do?" he said.

"Once you distracted the ankylosaur, I tied a bowline into the end of the rope by the cliff. Just before I jumped I hooked a foot into the loop."

"You're lucky you didn't yank your foot off."

"I know how long to make a safety line. There was no risk at all."

Grant looked over the edge at the splattered dinosaur at the base of the cliff. "Except to it."

"Ready to head down at a slower rate than the dinosaur did?"

"I was ready days ago."

CHAPTER TWENTY-EIGHT

The descent took over five hours. Five hours and thirty-two minutes. Grant knew precisely because he counted every minute until his feet were again on a piece of ground more than a few centimeters wide.

They'd let their packs dangle several meters below them on short lengths of rope so that the packs wouldn't throw them off balance. As soon as his touched the ground, Grant had to restrain himself from jumping the last few meters after it.

Janaina had tied a rope safety harness around him that circumnavigated his waist then wrapped uncomfortably between and around his legs. He untied it first thing and prayed that his manhood hadn't suffered any permanent damage from the compression.

Janaina hopped down beside him from two meters up.

"See, easy as cake."

"Easy as *pie*, and it wasn't. I know for a fact that cliff was trying to kill me."

She tapped him on the chest. "Well, it did a poor job of it."

Around him, the trees were all familiar looking. Insects buzzed and chirped around them. Travel a hundred meters and he was back in the 21st century. A trail snaked away into the jungle.

"That should take us to the river," Janaina said. "And the river takes us home."

A short time later, the trail ended at the river. Narrow sandy banks ran along both sides. The water ran swift.

"Is this normal?" Grant said.

He pointed up into a tree. A dugout canoe lay wedged between two branches. Moss grew along one side.

"Oh! Wonderful. That is a local design. It was probably lost in a flood and washed down river to get stuck here. We just need to get it down and that will be our ticket home."

Grant looked at the rippling river. Both overgrown banks appeared untouched by man.

"We might be the first non-natives to ever travel down this section of the river," he said.

"Sounds like that might turn into an adventure," Janaina said.

Grant had an unsettling feeling that it most certainly would.

AFTERWORD

Since the first excavation of their fossils, dinosaurs have captured people's imaginations. It seems that every boy, and many girls, go through a "dinosaur phase" where the animals become an obsession. Tens of thousands of people never grow out of it and have fashioned careers trying to find more clues and extrapolate more understanding about these extinct creatures. Jules Verne fantasized about finding some; the *Jurassic Park* films dreamed of recreating them.

Dinosaurs ruled my primary school life. I had books about them and toys that represented them. I wish I still had my View-Master reels of three-dimensional dinosaurs and my battery powered T-Rex that walked across the room with glowing red eyes. A middle-school visit to the dinosaur exhibit at New York City's Museum of Natural History was such an anticipated event that I'm certain I drove my parents insane talking about it for weeks before and after. Standing in the shadows of the bones of those creatures was thrilling.

So, fresh off surviving his ordeal in *Cavern of the Damned*, I thought it would be great to let Dr. Grant Coleman do what I'd always dreamed of—go face to face with some dinosaurs.

The ones in the story are mostly true to life. The phoberomys are a species discovered in South America that lived about eight million years ago. The ankylosaurus is a pretty commonly known dinosaur, but I added its carnivorous activities because plant eaters wrapped in defensive armor usually are not the threatening type. It really did have a huge bony club at the end of its tail, which had to give many predators pause.

The pterosaurs are an amalgamation of many species that have been excavated over the centuries. Whether they flew or just glided, whether they just perched or actually walked, all is up for conjecture, and the conventional wisdom seems to shift a lot. What they definitely didn't have are ovipositors in the end of their bills.

The giant ants are based on the normal-sized version we like to spray with a can of Raid. Soldier ants and weaver ants and ants making bridges all happen in the real world, though not all coming from the same colony. And before you whine that the spiracles that allow for ants' passive breathing through their skin means they'd never get so big, I will direct you to Grant hearing them use active respiration. Oh, and I'd remind you that this is fiction.

The mind-controlling larvae in the ants' skulls are also based on real science. Do an internet search on the emerald cockroach wasp for a really fascinating example of a wasp doing this with venom. Then there's a Costa Rican wasp that lays eggs on orb spiders and the larvae make the spider spin a strange, new web. And don't miss hairworms infecting dry land crickets with a larva that drives the crickets into water, where the cricket drowns, but the hairworm can emerge and live on. Who needs scary fiction when Mother Nature serves up stuff like this?

And finally, there really are Stone Age tribes deep in the Amazon that have had no or limited contact with the 21st century world. Debate rages on about how to treat these pockets of our distant past. Isolation, integration, or something in between? Like Heisenberg's principle, there is the likelihood that even our act of observation will forever alter their culture. Real-world Janainas champion their cause.

Special thanks goes out to Beta Readers Extraordinaire Donna Fitzpatrick, Teresa Robeson, Deborah Grace, and Belinda Whitney. They are sworn to secrecy about the horrendous errors they pointed out.

What's in store for Grant Coleman? Who knows. But that's a pretty long river he'll need to navigate to get back to civilization. It might get dangerous.

Russell James
October 2017

CHECK OUT OTHER GREAT DINOSAUR THRILLERS

JURASSIC ISLAND
by Viktor Zarkov

Guided by satellite photos and modern technology a ragtag group of survivalists and scientists travel to an uncharted island in the remote South Indian Ocean. Things go to hell in a hurry once the team reaches the island and the massive megalodon that attacked their boats is only the beginning of their desperate fight for survival.

Nothing could have prepared billionaire explorer Joseph Thornton and washed up archaeologist Christopher "Colt" McKinnon for the terrifying prehistoric creatures that wait for them on JURASSIC ISLAND!

K-REX
by L.Z. Hunter

Deep within the Congo jungle, Circuitz Mining employs mercenaries as security for its Coltan mining site. Armed with assault rifles and decades of experience, nothing should go wrong. However, the dangers within the jungle stretch beyond venomous snakes and poisonous spiders. There is more to fear than guerrillas and vicious animals. Undetected, something lurks under the expansive treetop canopy . . .

Something ancient.

Something dangerous.

Kasai Rex!

SEVEREDPRESS

CHECK OUT OTHER GREAT DINOSAUR THRILLERS

SPINOSAURUS
by Hugo Navikov

Brett Russell is a hunter of the rarest game. His targets are cryptids, animals denied by science. But they are well known by those living on the edges of civilization, where monsters attack and devour their animals and children and lay ruin to their shantytowns.

When a shadowy organization sends Brett to the Congo in search of the legendary dinosaur cryptid Kasai Rex, he will face much more than a terrifying monster from the past.

Spinosaurus is a dinosaur thriller packed with intrigue, action and giant prehistoric predators.

LAND OF DEATH
by Eric S Brown & Alex Laybourne

A group of American soldiers, fleeing an organized attack on their base camp in the Middle East, encounter a storm unlike anything they've seen before. When the storm subsides, they wake up to find themselves no longer in the desert and perhaps not even on Earth. The jungle they've been deposited in is a place ruled by prehistoric creatures long extinct. Each day is a struggle to survive as their ammo begins to run low and virtually everything they encounter, in this land they've been hurled into, is a deadly threat.

CHECK OUT OTHER GREAT DINOSAUR THRILLERS

WRITTEN IN STONE
by David Rhodes

Charles Dawson is trapped 100 million years in the past. Trying to survive from day to day in a world of dinosaurs he devises a plan to change his fate. As he begins to write messages in the soft mud of a nearby stream, he can only hope they will be found by someone who can stop his time travel. Professor Ron Fontana and Professor Ray Taggit, scientists with opposing views, each discover the fossilized messages. While attempting to save Charles, Professor Fontana, his daughter Lauren and their friend Danny are forced to join Taggit and his group of mercenaries. Taggit does not intend to rescue Charles Dawson, but to force Dawson to travel back in time to gather samples for Taggit's fame and fortune. As the two groups jump through time they find they must work together to make it back alive as this fast-paced thriller climaxes at the very moment the age of dinosaurs is ending.

HARD TIME
by Alex Laybourne

Rookie officer Peter Malone and his heavily armed team are sent on a deadly mission to extract a dangerous criminal from a classified prison world. A Kruger Correctional facility where only the hardest, most vicious criminals are sent to fend for themselves, never to return.

But when the team come face to face with ancient beasts from a lost world, their mission is changed. The new objective: Survive.